SOPHOCLES

THE THEBAN PLAYS

KING OEDIPUS

OEDIPUS AT COLONUS

ANTIGONE

-

TRANSLATED BY E. F. WATLING

PENGUIN BOOKS

BALTIMORE · MARYLAND

Penguin Books Ltd, Harmondsworth, Middlesex, England
Penguin Books Inc., 7110 Ambassador Road, Baltimore, Maryland 21207, U.S.A.
Penguin Books Australia Ltd, Ringwood, Victoria, Australia

—

This translation first published 1947
Reprinted 1949, 1951, 1952, 1953, 1954, 1955, 1956, 1957, 1958, 1959 (twice),
1960, 1961, 1962, 1963, 1964, 1965 (twice), 1966, 1967 (twice), 1968, 1969

—

Copyright © E. F. Watling, 1947

—

Made and printed in Great Britain
by Richard Clay (The Chaucer Press) Ltd,
Bungay, Suffolk
Set in Monotype Bembo

—

*The terms for the performance of these plays may
be obtained from the League of Dramatists,
84 Drayton Gardens, SW10,
to whom all applications for
permission should
be made*

CONTENTS

*

INTRODUCTION

I

SOPHOCLES the Athenian was born in 496 B.C. and lived ninety years. A memoir written by an anonymous scholar of a later age – perhaps two hundred years after the poet's death – gives us a picture of his life which we may take to be substantially true in outline and in spirit, though some of its circumstantial details may be apocryphal: a picture of a childhood spent under the best influences of a prosperous and enlightened home, a youth educated in a harmonious physical and intellectual discipline and endowed with grace and accomplishment, a manhood devoted to the service of the state in art and public affairs, and an old age regarded with affectionate respect.

He lived through a cycle of events spatially narrow, no doubt, in the scale of national and global history, but without parallel in intensity of action and emotion, and of lasting significance in the procession of human achievement. At his birth, Athens was still in the infancy of her life as a free democracy, making her first experiments with the new machinery of popular government. During his boyhood she was defending that life and liberty, and those of Greece and the Europe of the future, against the aggression of the power-state of Persia. In his sixteenth year he was the chosen leader and symbol of Athenian youth in the ceremonial celebration of the decisive victory of Salamis. Through most of the fifty comparatively peaceful years during which Athens created and enjoyed the richness and breadth of a free social life and culture, Sophocles contributed to the expression of that culture in the theatre which was its prime temple, performing also in his course the public duties which were as much the province of the artist as of the man of action. From his sixty-fifth year another struggle for existence engaged and drained the forces of Athens and her miniature empire, when in the so-called Peloponnesian War all Greece was divided by contrary ideals of statecraft and opposing ambitions for power. He died as that struggle was drawing to a close, leaving Athens materially exhausted and spiritually wrecked by the physical and moral strains of the conflict.

For first-hand acquaintance with the life and spirit of this momentous age we naturally turn to its surviving literature; and of this, apart from the two major historical works of Herodotus and Thucydides, by far the greatest bulk, and incomparably the greatest in range and power, is the work of the three tragedians, Aeschylus, Sophocles, and Euripides, and the comedian, Aristophanes. The lyric poetry of Greece belongs mainly to the seventh and sixth centuries B.C., that of the fifth century being traditional rather than contemporary or progressive in spirit; while the full flowering of prose in oratory and philosophy is not to be seen until the fourth century. What then, was this Athenian theatre, into which was poured so much of the creative power of the age, and whose literature, it seems, is almost all that is left to us with which to fill out the factual narratives of the historians?

Negatively – to rid ourselves of the associations of modern 'theatre' – we must determine what it was *not*. It was not a place of daily or nightly resort and entertainment. It was not a medium in which any ingenious story-teller could make a living by the invention of novel, amusing, or exciting fictions to tickle the fancy of a chance audience. It was not a place in which to hold the mirror up to life in all its superficial and ephemeral detail. Even its comedy, which drew upon the contemporary social and political scene for subject-matter, did so only to add a topical spice to a highly stylised and largely conventional product. But tragedy, with which we are here concerned, touched the deepest centres of man's individual and corporate consciousness.

Tragedies were presented in the Athenian theatre at certain annual festivals. At the principal one, held in the spring, the whole population, swelled by large numbers of visiting strangers, was assembled on a number of successive days, and for the greater part of each day, in an open-air theatre accommodating about 17,000 spectators, to witness a cycle of dramatic performances presented amid high civic splendour and religious ritual. On the practitioners of this art, therefore, rested a solemn responsibility, and for its worthy performance the rewards, in esteem and possibly in material value, were substantial. Competition was the order of the day, and was not felt to be incongruous with the religious dignity of the occasion. Before a tragedy could be performed at all, it had to pass the scrutiny of a selection board, and its acceptance for production already conferred a high honour on the author. In performance it competed with the work of two other chosen authors, and the victory in the whole contest was awarded by the votes of a panel of adjudicators, influenced, no doubt, to some degree by the reactions of the audience. For the purposes of this contest, the work of each author consisted of a group of four plays – three tragedies, either independent of each other or forming a 'trilogy' on a connected theme, and a 'satyr-play' in lighter vein. Such were the basic conditions of the dramatist's art, and within them was established a code of technique and convention of which more must now be said – though the new reader may, at this point, prefer (and not unwisely) to turn to the plays themselves and form his own impressions of them before seeking the answers to such questions as they will probably suggest.

II

The origins of the art of drama, in Greece as elsewhere, lie far beyond the reach of literary or even archaeological evidence. At its roots lie not only the human instinct for narrative and impersonation, but also the instinct for the ritualistic expression and interpretation of the power of natural forces, the cycle of life and death, and the nexus of past, present, and future. By the time the art emerges into anything like historical daylight, it is evident that the elements of dance and song are essential to its nature and that its prime function is the expression of the feelings and reasonings excited by man's battles with the eternal forces that appear to govern his life – in Sophoclean words 'the encounters of man with more than man'. These two character-istics – the choric element and the religious note – survive throughout the great period of Greek tragedy. In the earliest plays of Aeschylus the strictly dramatic element is hardly greater than, for instance, that of a modern oratorio; the play is a poem recited or sung by a 'chorus' with one or two 'characters' to personify its leading themes; and even with Euripides the in-novator, the Chorus, though often standing aloof from the now more highly developed plot and action, is still the unifying and commenting interpreter of the drama. In common parlance a dramatic performance was as often called a 'chorus' as a 'drama'.

Sophocles stands midway between Aeschylus and Euripides in this respect. For him, the dramatic action is vital and to a great extent realistic, but the Chorus is also essential to the play both in its capacity as actor in the events of the drama, and as 'presenter' of its dominating theme in lyric terms; and a par-ticularly subtle and interesting feature of his technique is the way in which the Chorus, distinctly characterised as 'Elders of Thebes', 'People of Colonus', and so on, bridge the foot-lights, as it were, between spectator and stage, their presence and participation in the acted events heightening the vividness and urgency of the action. With them we, the audience, are citizens of Thebes, witnesses of the passion of Oedipus, the mar-tyrdom of Antigone; whose conflicts must not only be fought out, but must be fought out in public, submitted to the scru-tiny and judgment of their fellow-men. Sometimes, indeed, this double function of the Chorus, as actor and as commentator, leads, we may think, to a somewhat too palpable inconsistency. The Chorus of *Antigone*, in their dramatic character, must ex-press a submissive, if rather unenthusiastic, loyalty to their king, Creon, and are heard to reprove Antigone as having 'gone to the outermost limit of daring, and stumbled against Law enthroned'; 'authority,' they opine, 'cannot afford to

connive at disobedience'. But in the greater detachment of
their lyric utterances they are instinctively aware, as we must
be, that the truth of the situation, and of the tragedy, lies deeper
than that. For it is here a question of two stubborn wills, each
loyal to a principle good in itself, but each pressing that loyalty
with ruthless single-mindedness to the point at which it breaks
against the other, and on both the disaster falls. Yet there is a
plausibility and a dramatic necessity in this convention. The
tragedy, whatever its subject, is *our* tragedy. We, like the
Chorus, are both in it and spectators of it. And while the tragedy is played out, we identify ourselves now with this character and now with that – inconsistent, vacillating mortals that
we are. But the tragedy is not fully played out, the story not
fully told, until we have looked the whole matter squarely in
the face and commented on it, so far as lies in us, truthfully,
impartially, without passion, bias, or self-deception.

It is, then, in the Chorus as persons, and in their more imper-
sonal lyric interludes, that we shall chiefly observe that religious approach to the dramatic theme which, as we have said, is
an essential characteristic of Greek Tragedy. It remains to notice some further consequences of this religious approach. The
Greek dramatists could, no doubt, if they had been so minded,
have constructed plays of 'ordinary life' in which the tragic
aspects of man's ambition or perversity should be starkly depicted against a contemporary background. But dramatic convention grows and changes slowly, and the fact remains that it
was taken as axiomatic that the play should tell some already
established story of the legendary and heroic past. (The few
exceptions to this rule only demonstrate the unsuitability of
any other kind of theme for such treatment as the conventions
demanded.) Indeed, it was not necessary that the play should
'tell a story' self-contained and complete. Since the audience
was already in possession of the main facts of the story, the
way was prepared for the dramatist to come swiftly to whatever situation in it he chose for the exposition of his theme.

Some element of narrative, of course, remained, as well as much scope for originality in the ordering of the incidents within the chosen field; but the attention of the audience was not primarily to be held by the factor of suspense or the desire to 'see what happens'. And this was the most fitting condition for an artform which was to invite not a passing curiosity but profound contemplation of eternal truths. In addition, on the technical side, it gave the dramatist that powerful and subtle weapon of 'dramatic irony', which Sophocles used with especial skill, whereby the audience can judge every speech and action of the play in the light of their previous knowledge of the situation. We are to imagine, then, an Athenian audience listening – for it was more a matter of listening than of looking, even though the *décor*, within its conventional limits, was carried out with lavish care and expense – listening to a tragedy somewhat in the attitude of a Christian audience at a Nativity or Passion play, familiar with the accepted version of the story and thus the more ready to grasp, and to criticise, the particular interpretation offered by the author, and to be struck by any out-of-the-way incident or novel emphasis in his treatment of the subject. It may reasonably be added, without contradiction of the above principle, that part of the function of the drama was to keep alive the old stories, and that some, the youngest, of the audience, must often have found in the theatre their first introduction to them – nor would they have been disappointed, in most cases, of a clear and exciting tale.

III

The three plays included in this volume are derived, it will be seen, from one cycle of legend – that concerning the royal house of Thebes – and may be read, with the connecting narrative which will be found in its place, as a continuous saga. But with a caution. The plays were not written or produced in the order in which they are here placed – the order of the narrative – and they belong to widely different periods in the poet's life. Their probable dates are: *Antigone*, 442–441 B.C.; *King Oedipus*, 429–420; *Oedipus at Colonus*, 401 (after the poet's death). The series, therefore, cannot have formed a 'trilogy' in the sense already referred to; nor from internal evidence should we have supposed that it did. Beyond the fact that each of the three plays deals with a situation in the Oedipodean family history, there is no unity of theme or treatment between them, and, except for the obvious links of fact connecting them, each constitutes a fresh approach to a distinct and self-contained problem. A minor detail, but significant, is that the respective ages of the persons concerned cannot be harmonized with any probability. Creon, who must be at least as old as his nephew, Oedipus, and speaks of himself as, like him, an old man in *Oedipus at Colonus*, would be still older in *Antigone*; but his character in the latter play is that of a vigorous middle-aged father of a youthful son, who is betrothed to the still youthful Antigone.

In *Antigone* (to take them now in the order of the poet's thought) we are concerned with a single, and comparatively simple, conflict. A king, in full and sincere consciousness of his responsibility for the integrity of the state, has, for an example against treason, made an order of ruthless punishment upon a traitor and rebel – an order denying the barest rites of sepulture to his body, and therefore of solace to his soul. A woman, for whom political expediency takes second place, by a long way, to compassion and piety, has defied the order and is condemned to death. Here is conflict enough, and tragedy – not in the martyrdom of obvious right under obvious wrong, but in the far more bitter, and at the same time more exhilarating, contest between two passionately held principles of right, each partly justifiable, and each to a degree (though one more than the other) vitiated by stubborn blindness to the merits of the opposite. But there is more: between these two antagonists stands a third character, in whom their tragedy, and that of the whole situation, is personified and brought to a single focus – a young man, betrothed to the woman, whom he honours for her courage and piety, and son to the king, whom he has respected and longs to go on respecting for his fatherhood and for his office. To see statecraft misdirected into blasphemous defiance of piety is for him (and for the Athenian audience) the greater tragedy; the sacrifice of a well-meaning woman, the less. Thus the king's final humiliation and chastening, through the loss of his son, is of higher dramatic significance than the fate of the woman. This triangular tragedy, of the woman ruled by conscience, the king too confident in his authority, and the young man tormented by conflicting loyalties, it is the function of the Chorus to resolve, gradually but in the end uncompromisingly, by appeal to God's law, which alone can hold the scales between opposing and imperfect human wills. All else (to this conclusion the successive choral odes point with cumulative force) – intellect, ambition, power, even love itself – draws mankind as often to evil as to good:

> 'Of happiness the crown
> And chiefest part
> Is wisdom, and to hold
> The gods in awe.
> This is the law
> That, seeing the stricken heart
> Of pride brought down,
> We learn when we are old.'

Returning to the Theban legend in the maturity of his powers, Sophocles produced in *King Oedipus* the masterpiece of his life's work, so far as we can judge from the seven plays surviving out of the hundred or more ascribed to his pen. This is the judgment also of Aristotle, who has this play constantly at his elbow as the perfect type of tragic composition. In brief, its greatness lies in the combination of a faultlessly articulated plot with the profoundest insight into human motive and circumstance. Formally a story of the impact of quite fortuitous mischance upon a man of no exceptional faults or virtues, it lays bare, with a ruthless sincerity worthy of its own protagonist, the pitfalls lying about the path of man, into which those very unexceptional faults or virtues may at a touch overbalance him, at the bidding of some incalculable chance, and out of which he must raise himself, chastened and ennobled, by the 'greatness in the soul' which alone makes him a match for the eternal powers. The anthropological and religious implications of the story offer fruitful fields of research and speculation to the expert inquirer. The average reader will be well enough rewarded by a study of the more universal human issues of the drama. Oedipus, too complacent in his prosperity, too confident of his sufficiency, too ready to take offence or to impute blame when 'rattled' by the approach of trouble; Oedipus, unshirking in the performance of a self-appointed unpleasant task, unflinching in quest of the truth at whatever cost of terrible self-revelation; Oedipus driven to the summit of passion by agony of body and soul, and returning at the last to humility and selfless resignation: this vast and living portrait of man, surrounded by a group of subsidiary portraits no less vital, has no equal in the Greek, nor perhaps in any other, theatre. The Chorus, fellow-citizens desperately implicated in the awful happenings, are more than ever closely tied to the action, and their moods move swiftly with the march of events. Bewildered and apprehensive, they have little respite for calm reflection or reasoned judgment, and even their final words seem only to deepen the hopeless gloom. What more constructive 'moral' they would draw for us is implied, rather than stated, in their moods of apprehension lest divine law should after all be found wanting and a lurking spirit of defiance be vindicated by the event. This worst calamity at least is averted.

'Then learn that mortal man must always look to his ending,
And none can be called happy until that day when he carries
His happiness down to the grave in peace.'

These closing words of *King Oedipus* themselves suggest a sequel; but it was only in the closing years of his own long life that Sophocles completed the story with the legend of the passing of the aged hero. Oedipus does not indeed die happy, but in *Oedipus at Colonus* he is a different man. Though resigned by long endurance to the hardness of his physical lot, the consciousness of defilement coupled with moral innocence has in no way softened his daemonic temper, which blazes out with the old fury in denunciation of his rebellious son and deceitful uncle; but it has brought him to a sense of his symbolic sacredness, as a person set apart, a sufferer in whom others may find redemption. Therefore a special and wonderful end is reserved for him, a passing 'without grief or agony, more marvellous than that of any other man'.

The mood of the play is a singular blend of harshness and serenity, with slow-moving action and a somewhat static plot, and a strongly-marked ritual element which presents some difficulty to the modern reader. The whole is sweetened with the fragrant local atmosphere of a spot long hallowed and cherished in Athenian lore, no other than the poet's own birthplace, the 'white Colonus', to which he pays his farewell tribute in one of his most picturesque odes.

IV

'Hard to analyse, impossible to translate' – such, says Dr J. T. Sheppard (*Greek Tragedy*) is 'Sophoclean language at its best'. In the face of such an admonition from a supreme authority (who has himself produced a masterly version of *King Oedipus*) a new translator may well search his heart for an excuse for his audacity. In the versions which I now offer (largely, I hope, to new and unprejudiced readers) I have taken as my first aim the production of a readable, and actable, dramatic text, not a line-for-line, word-for-word transcription of the original. Inaccuracies are, I hope, as few as is humanly possible; but an accurate rendering is not a translation. The problem of finding English substitutes for Greek idiom and terminology is difficult enough in prose, more difficult in verse, and most difficult of all in drama. For here we require not only the lucidity of prose and the formality of verse, but a 'personality' in every speech that will 'get it across' to the audience as the living utterance of a living character. What character? And in what situation? If there is no English equivalent of a Greek demigod, soothsayer, or messenger, and still less of the social background against which they stand, in what sort of English dress are they to be presented? We can only adopt a substitution, which on historical grounds will be more or less misleading, of such idiom and vocabulary as will create a sufficiently convincing atmosphere. In fact, of course, no translation is free of this difficulty – the difficulty of non-corresponding terms. It would be an exaggeration to say that no Greek word has an exact equivalent in English; we are on sufficiently safe ground with such words as *eye, night, tree, water,* and shall probably not get into serious difficulties with *husband, house, battle, dance,* though the possibility of misrepresentation is here already within sight. But with *god, king, city, law, virtue, priest, sin, honour,* and a host of kindred words very prevalent in tragedy, we enter a sphere in which the English vocabulary is clothed with associations which are at least partly, and sometimes wholly, different from the Greek. For this reason there are those who hold that you cannot call Oedipus 'King', or Zeus 'God', without falsifying the social and religious background of the original. What, then, are you to do? For the resources of English are not inexhaustible.

Considering the problem with special reference to drama, I have argued thus. The reader of the printed page may take his own time to consider the implications of this or that expression, and may in due course accustom himself to an unfamiliar terminology. But the listener cannot so pause; his understanding and emotion must respond at the instant, and must not be baulked or side-tracked by an unnecessary puzzle; nor must the actor be hampered by having to convey meaning and fervour through a too unfamiliar word-medium – rather he is to be helped by the use, even at the cost of inexactitude, of such terms as will most immediately strike the right dramatic note.

(Some Shakespearean anachronisms are of this order; we would not exchange the 'hats' and 'clocks' of *Julius Caesar* for their more correct Roman equivalents, if any.) Now every listener may be presumed to understand, at least in some degree, that a 'king' in ancient Greece is not the equivalent of a king in modern England. For that matter King Richard II is not equivalent to King George VI; nor the King of Great Britain to the King of Abyssinia. What a 'king' in ancient Greece actually was, can be learnt only by an intensive study of the literature and archaeology, and we do not answer any questions by calling him 'tyrant', 'prince', 'governor', or 'lord' – when in fact he was probably something more like a wealthy landowner. All that is necessary for the play is that he should be recognised as a 'great one' in virtue of his own power of command and, it may be, of the election of his townsmen. And of all the possible alternatives, I think that 'king', as being at once the widest and most dignified term, is the least objectionable.

The question of 'god' is perhaps more controversial. But again, no one supposes that the Greek 'god', or 'God', though he had many names, was ever Jehovah, Allah, or Vishnu. And I hold that in certain contexts a listener will be less distracted or jarred, and the dramatic 'temperature' more truly registered, by the word 'God' than by the word 'Zeus'. At the same time there are distinctions that must be made; and the following observations may serve to explain some apparent contradictions or inconsistencies.

(1) 'God' I consider to be permissible, and the truest rendering, where the notion is of the great invisible source of moral law or unseen arbiter of human destiny (*Antigone* 450: 'That order did not come from God').

(2) 'The gods' is sometimes similar in significance to the foregoing, but it is also used in a lower anthropomorphic sense (*Oedipus at Colonus* 607: 'Only the gods have ageless and deathless life').

(3) 'The god', though not very happy in English, is unavoidable where the reference is to a particular god – usually Apollo,

who communicates his messages to man through his oracle, and ministers (*King Oedipus* 77: ' Whatever the god requires it shall be done').

(4) 'A god' will usually be one of an indeterminate range of nameless powers, mostly of evil.

(5) 'Zeus', and some other names, must be left unaltered where the differentiation is obviously necessary, and where the context does not require that degree of real intensity for which I reserve the term 'God'. It will be noticed also that such a name is sometimes taken almost 'in vain', as in *Oedipus at Colonus* 310, where Antigone, at the unexpected arrival of her sister, exclaims 'O Zeus! What do I see?' 'O God' is here clearly impossible.

In the matter of idiom and style my principle has been much the same. A literal translation can only result in prose – or worse, a strained versification – which may faithfully (and rightly, for some purposes) preserve the quite un-English constructions and thought-processes of the original, but cannot possibly be spoken as living English. For straightforward reading, and for acting, we need contemporary English, not Greek in an Elizabethan or Victorian disguise. What looks like a cliché or proverbial saying must be rendered by the most appropriate contemporary equivalent. Outbursts of passionate or hasty speech on the one hand, and casual commonplaces on the other, must fall into whatever form will come with the right accent from the actor's lips. When all is said and done, an ancient Greek play can never be a modern English one, and some degree of incongruity is inescapable; but in stage performance, and to some extent in reading, we can and should recapture most of the dramatic force and characterisation of the original, and these cannot possibly be preserved in a dead or imitative idiom.

I would not wish anyone to imagine that in these, or any other, versions he will find the whole Sophocles and nothing but Sophocles. Translation inevitably omits, or transmutes, something of its original, and cannot escape importing something that is alien to it. At best it can ease the opening of doors that would otherwise remain, for some, permanently closed; it cannot transmit the whole quality of what lies behind those doors.

V

The proper place for drama is in the theatre; and, like most great drama, Greek tragedy will survive transplantation into a theatrical climate quite different from that in which it was first reared. To anyone contemplating the production of any of these plays my advice would be that he should not be unduly burdened, and certainly not be daunted, by a too scrupulous awareness of the physical conditions of the ancient Greek theatre. That theatre was a vast open-air arena, provided with a dancing-place (*orchestra*) in which the Chorus moved and chanted; a platform for the actors, probably raised by a few steps above the *orchestra* and communicating with it; and a building which afforded both a retiring-place for the actors and a background for their performance. The dress and action of the players were designed in formal style for long-distance effect; the actor wore a mask which depicted with broad and exaggerated emphasis the dominant characteristics of his rôle. In our own time and place open-air acting is a doubtful pro-position at best, and the chances of our ever being able to ap-preciate, or achieve, a faithful replica of an ancient Greek per-formance are remote – though there have been some interest-ing experiments. The modern producer will have other advan-tages – chiefly a more intimate relation between stage and audience, providing greater scope for the abundant subtlety of speech which the dialogue affords. The use of a drop-curtain will not be out of place (though the play should usually be pre-sented without an interval), and will simplify and enhance, for instance, the opening scene of *King Oedipus*, where a 'crowd' is discovered on-stage (an unusual opening, incidentally, for the Greek theatre, where they must have 'entered'). Settings can be either simple or elaborate, according to taste or opportunity; for most Greek plays a dignified central entrance, preferably approached by a step or two, is the minimum requirement; side entrances are also presumed, one leading to the immediate neighbourhood of the 'city', the other to more distant country. One of the plays in this volume, *Oedipus at Colonus*, requires a rustic scene. It is in connection with such as this, no doubt, that Sophocles became known as 'the inventor of scene-painting'; whatever this involved, we cannot suppose that it implies anything approaching realism, which would have been as disastrous on the Greek stage as in any modern 'little theatre'. The Greeks were doubtless quite as capable of using their imagination as we are.

The Chorus may be as large or small as convenience indicates; fifteen was the regular number in Sophocles's day, but as few as five will serve. Large or small, it is essential that their words should be intelligible; the choral odes should be spoken in unison – or distributed among the speakers – rather than sung to any musical setting in the modern formula. Incidental music, on single instruments of wood-wind or string, should be confined to short interludes marking the passage of time or the transition between chorus and dialogue. Nor should audibility of speech be sacrificed to any complicated 'eurhythmic' movements, though there may be some place for stylised grouping and posture. On the speaking of the verse in general, a word of caution may be desirable. The traditional iambic line of the Shakespearean pattern comes easily to the reader, but for that reason may as easily become monotonous to the ear. I have used, for the most part, a much 'resolved' form of iambic line which allows a greater elasticity of construction while preserving the basic five-stress rhythm; the proper 'pointing' of a line is thus not always obvious to the reader at first sight, but when rightly delivered will be found to maintain the rhythm and confirm the sense.

Recent experiments in contemporary verse-drama have accustomed actors and audiences to a form of naturalistic, yet rhythmical, speech, which is probably nearer to the pattern of Greek dramatic verse than the more formal rhetoric of our older classic drama. It is this development in modern drama that has made possible the type of diction at which I have aimed in the versions here offered to new generations of readers and actors.

December 1946.   E. F. W.

The text followed is mainly that of Jebb
(Cambridge; O.T. 1893, O.C. 1889, Ant. 1891).

THE THEBAN LEGEND

The place called Thebes lay in the central plain of Boeotia, part of the narrow tongue of land joining the Athenian country to the more northerly mainland. Here, under the guidance of the oracle of Delphi, a city was first founded by Cadmus, son of Agenor and brother of that Europa whom Zeus courted in the likeness of a bull. Misfortune befell him even before his city was established, for all the trusty companions who should have been his first citizens were devoured by a fierce dragon which inhabited a neighbouring glen. But Cadmus was a match for the dragon and at one stroke laid him dead. Again the word of Heaven guided him, and he was instructed to sow the dragon's teeth in the ground prepared for his future city; from which seed there instantly sprang up a tribe of giants so fierce and fully armed that a deadly combat immediately broke out between them. At length but five remained alive, and these offering their submission to Cadmus became the founders and fathers of the Thebes to be.

Cadmus begat Polydorus, and Polydorus begat Labdacus, and Labdacus begat Laius; and to Laius and his wife Jocasta a son was born. Before even a name had been given to this infant – indeed, by some accounts, before he was born – his life was clouded with the presage of disaster; for Apollo's oracle had nothing but ill to foretell of him: he was destined one day to kill his father, and to become his own mother's husband. Could any mortal device be proof against the god's prediction? Could any mortal be so presumptuous as to try to thwart it? Laius and Jocasta would so presume. One way alone offered any hope – more than hope, certainty. The child should not live. They would not indeed take upon themselves the guilt of infanticide, but they would deliver the child to a servant of theirs, a shepherd, with orders to abandon it on the mountain-side, its feet cruelly pierced with an iron pin, so that it might not even crawl to safety.

This was done. But still the word of Apollo – and human compassion – prevailed. For the shepherd had not the heart to leave the child to perish; instead he entrusted it to a fellow-labourer, a Corinthian shepherd, beseeching him to take it away beyond the borders of Thebes and rear it as his own. The Corinthian, a servant of Polybus, King of Corinth, in due course brought the child to his royal master, who, being childless, gladly welcomed the infant and adopted it as his own, giving it the name of Oedipus (Swollen-foot) in commiseration for its painful treatment.

Oedipus grew to manhood, the honoured Prince of Corinth and loved foster-son of those whom he supposed to be his true parents. But by chance he came to hear, again from the mouth of Apollo's ministers, the terrible prediction concerning him. Again, as his parents had done, he sought to give lie to the oracle. He fled from Corinth, resolved never again to set eyes on his supposed father and mother as long as they lived. His wanderings brought him to Thebes, where now all was calamity and confusion. King Laius had been killed by an unknown traveller on a lonely road; the city was in the grip of a deadly monster, the Sphinx, who pitted her ferocity against the wits of man, destroying all who failed to answer her cunning riddle: and none could answer it. But in Oedipus the creature met her match. He answered her riddle and destroyed her power, and so was received joyfully into Thebes as her king and heir to the house and fortune; a happy man, a wise and resourceful man, and (save for one sharp encounter on his journey from Corinth to Thebes) a man of peace. He married Jocasta; and sons and daughters were born to them.

There passed some fifteen years of seeming prosperity. But beneath the deceptive surface a hideous depth of shame and infamy lay concealed. The gods could no longer brook in silence the affront of Oedipus's unwitting sins. Pestilence and famine brought Thebes once more to the verge of utter extinction. In their despair her citizens cried to their king for yet more proofs of his infallible resource, and to their gods, chief among them Apollo, for light and healing in their wretchedness.

[Here the play of KING OEDIPUS begins]

KING OEDIPUS

*

CHARACTERS

Oedipus, *King of Thebes*
Jocasta, *wife of Oedipus*
Creon, *brother of Jocasta*
Teiresias, *a blind prophet*
A Priest
A Messenger
A Shepherd
An Attendant
Chorus *of Theban elders*
King's *attendants*
Queen's *attendants*
Citizens *of Thebes*

*

Scene: Before the Royal Palace at Thebes.

In front of the King's Palace, upon the steps and around the altars which stand in the forecourt, are grouped numerous citizens of Thebes, sitting in attitudes of supplication.

Enter OEDIPUS *from the central door, attended.*

OEDIPUS: Children, new blood of Cadmus' ancient line –
What is the meaning of this supplication,
These branches and garlands, the incense filling the city,
These prayers for the healing of pain, these lamentations?
I have not thought it fit to rely on my messengers,
But am here to learn for myself – I, Oedipus,
Whose name is known afar.
(*To the* PRIEST.) You, reverend sir,
In right of age should speak for all of them.
What is the matter? Some fear? Something you desire?

I would willingly do anything to help you;
Indeed I should be heartless, were I to stop my ears
To a general petition such as this.

PRIEST: My lord and king: we are gathered here, as you see,
Young and old, from the tenderest chicks to the age-bent
seniors;
Priests – I of Zeus – and the pick of our young manhood.
More sit in the market-place, carrying boughs like these,
And around the twin altars of Pallas and the sacred embers
Of divination, beside the river of Ismenus.

You too have seen our city's affliction, caught
In a tide of death from which there is no escaping –
Death in the fruitful flowering of her soil;
Death in the pastures; death in the womb of woman;
And pestilence, a fiery demon gripping the city,
Stripping the house of Cadmus, to fatten hell
With profusion of lamentation.

If we come to you now, sir, as your suppliants,
I and these children, it is not as holding you
The equal of gods, but as the first of men,
Whether in the ordinary business of mortal life,
Or in the encounters of man with more than man.
It was you, we remember, a newcomer to Cadmus' town,
That broke our bondage to the vile Enchantress.
With no foreknowledge or hint that we could give,
But, as we truly believe, with the help of God,
You gave us back our life.

Now, Oedipus great and glorious, we seek
Your help again. Find some deliverance for us
By any way that god or man can show.
We know that experience of trials past gives strength
To present counsel. Therefore, O greatest of men,
Restore our city to life. Have a care for your fame.
Your diligence saved us once; let it not be said
That under your rule we were raised up only to fall.
Save, save our city, and keep her safe for ever.

Under the same bright star that gave us then
Good fortune, guide us into good to-day.
If you are to be our King, as now you are,
Be king of living men, not emptiness.
Surely there is no strength in wall or ship,
Where men are lacking and no life breathes within them.

OEDIPUS:
I grieve for you, my children. Believe me, I know
All that you desire of me, all that you suffer;
And while you suffer, none suffers more than I.
You have your several griefs, each for himself;
But my heart bears the weight of my own, and yours
And all my people's sorrows. I am not asleep.
I weep; and walk through endless ways of thought.
But I have not been idle; one thing I have already done –
The only thing that promised hope. My kinsman
Creon, the son of Menoeceus, has been sent
To the Pythian house of Apollo, to learn what act
Or word of mine could help you. This is the day
I reckoned he should return. It troubles me
That he is not already here. But when he comes,
Whatever the god requires, upon my honour
It shall be done.

PRIEST: Well said.
          (*He descries someone approaching from a distance.*)
And look! They are making signs
That Creon is on his way. Yes. He is here!

OEDIPUS (*looking also*): And with smiling face! O Apollo!
If his news is good!

PRIEST: It must be good; his head is crowned with bay
Full-berried; that is a sign.

OEDIPUS: We shall soon know ...
He can hear us now ... Royal brother! What news?
What message for us from the mouth of God?
                    Enter CREON.

CREON: Good news. That is to say that good may come

Even out of painful matters, if all goes well.

OEDIPUS: And the answer? You hold me between fear and
    hope. The answer?

CREON:
  I will tell you – if you wish me to speak in the presence of all.
  If not, let us go in.

OEDIPUS: Speak before all.
  Their plight concerns me now, more than my life.

CREON:
  This, then, is the answer, and this the plain command
  Of Phoebus our lord. There is an unclean thing,
  Born and nursed on our soil, polluting our soil,
  Which must be driven away, not kept to destroy us.

OEDIPUS:
  What unclean thing? And what purification is required?

CREON:
  The banishment of a man, or the payment of blood for blood.
  For the shedding of blood is the cause of our city's peril.

OEDIPUS:
  What blood does he mean? Did he say who it was that died?

CREON: We had a king, sir, before you came to lead us.
  His name was Laius.

OEDIPUS: I know. I never saw him.

CREON: He was killed. And clearly the meaning of the god's
    command
  Is that we bring the unknown killer to justice.

OEDIPUS:
  And where might *he* be? Where shall we hope to uncover
  The faded traces of that far-distant crime?

CREON: Here – the god said. Seek, and ye shall find.
  Unsought goes undetected.

OEDIPUS: Was it at home,
  Or in the field, or abroad on foreign soil,
  That Laius met his death, this violent death?

CREON: He left the country, as he said, on a pilgrimage;
  And from that day forth we never saw him again.

OEDIPUS: Was there no word, no fellow-traveller
  Who saw what happened, whose evidence could have been
      used?
CREON: All died; save one, who fled from the scene in terror,
  And had nothing to tell for certain – except one thing.
OEDIPUS:
  What was it? One thing might point the way to others,
  If once we could lay our hands on the smallest clue.
CREON: His story was that robbers – not one but many –
  Fell in with the King's party and put them to death.
OEDIPUS:
  Robbers would hardly commit such a daring outrage –
  Unless they were paid to do it by someone here.
CREON:
  That too was suggested. But in the troubles that followed
  No avenger came forward to punish the murderers.
OEDIPUS: What troubles? Surely none great enough to hinder
  A full inquiry into a royal death?
CREON:
  The Sphinx with her riddles forced us to turn our attention
  From insoluble mysteries to more immediate matters.
OEDIPUS:
  I will start afresh; and bring everything into the light.
  All praise to Phoebus – and thanks, for your part, to you –
  For thus pointing out our duty to the dead.
  You will find me as willing an ally as you could wish
  In the cause of God and our country. My own cause too –
  Not merely from a fellow-creature will I clear this taint,
  But from myself. The killer of Laius,
  Whoever he was, might think to turn his hand
  Against *me*; thus, serving Laius, I serve myself.
    Now, up from your seats, my children! Away with these
        boughs!
  Bring all the people of Cadmus here, and tell them
  There is nothing I will not do. Certain it is
  That by the help of God we stand – or fall.

OEDIPUS *goes into the Palace. A Messenger goes to summon the
people. The* PRIEST *dismisses the suppliants.*

PRIEST: Up, children. Now the King has promised us
All that we came to ask. Let us pray that Phoebus,
From whom the answer came, himself may come
To save and deliver us out of our heavy afflictions.

The suppliants disperse.

Enter the CHORUS *of Theban elders.*

CHORUS:
In Thebes, City of Light, from the Pythian House of Gold
The gracious voice of heaven is heard.
With fear my heart is riven, fear of what shall be told.
O Healer of Delos, hear!
Fear is upon us. What wilt thou do?
Things new, or old as the circling year?
Speak to us, Daughter of Golden Hope! Come, deathless
word!

Deathless Athena! First, Daughter of Zeus, on thee
We call; then on thy sister Queen
Artemis, over our city enthroned in her majesty;
And Phoebus, Lord of the Bow;
Show us again your threefold power
This hour, as in ages long ago.
From the fire and pain of pestilence save us and make us
[clean.

Sorrows beyond all telling –
Sickness rife in our ranks, outstripping
Invention of remedy – blight
On barren earth,
And barren agonies of birth –
Life after life from the wild-fire winging
Swiftly into the night.

Beyond all telling, the city
Reeks with the death in her streets, death-bringing.
None weeps, and her children die,

None by to pity.
Mothers at every altar kneel.
Golden Athena, come near to our crying!
Apollo, hear us and heal!

Not with the rattle of bronze, but loud around us
The battle is raging, swift the death-fiend flying.
Fling to the farthest corners of the sea,
Or to some bleak North bay,
The onset of his armoury!
Night's agony grows into tortured day.
Zeus, let thy thunders crush, thy lightning slay!

Slay with thy golden bow, Lycean! Slay him,
Artemis, over the Lycian hills resplendent!
Bacchus, our name-god, golden in the dance
Of Maenad revelry,
Euoe! thy fiery torch advance
To slay the Death-god, the grim enemy,
God whom all other gods abhor to see.

Enter OEDIPUS *from the Palace.*

OEDIPUS: You have prayed; and your prayers shall be answer-
    ed with help and release
If you will obey me, and are willing to put in hand
The remedy your distress requires. I speak
As a stranger, except by hearsay, to what has passed
And the story that has been told – without this clue
I should make but little headway in my search.
Therefore, as a citizen newly received among you,
It is to you, Thebans, I make this proclamation:
If any one of you knows whose hand it was
That killed Laius, the son of Labdacus,
Let him declare it fully, now, to me.
            (*He pauses: there is silence.*)
Or if any man's conscience is guilty, let him give himself up.
He will suffer the less. His fate will be nothing worse
Than banishment. No other harm will touch him.

(The hearers are still silent.)
Or, if some alien is known to have been the assassin,
Declare it. The informer shall have his reward of me,
As well as the thanks he will earn from all of you.
(Silence still.)
But – if you will not speak, and any man
Is found to be screening himself or another, in fear,
I here pronounce my sentence upon his head:
No matter who he may be, he is forbidden
Shelter or intercourse with any man
In all this country over which I rule;
From fellowship of prayer or sacrifice
Or lustral rite is excommunicated;
Expelled from every house, unclean, accursed,
In accordance with the word of the Pythian oracle.
Thus I shall have done my duty to the god,
And to the dead. And it is my solemn prayer
That the unknown murderer, and his accomplices,
If such there be, may wear the brand of shame
For their shameful act, unfriended, to their life's end.
Nor do I exempt myself from the imprecation:
If, with my knowledge, house or hearth of mine
Receive the guilty man, upon my head
Lie all the curses I have laid on others.
It is for you to see this faithfully carried out,
As in duty bound to me, and to the god,
And to our suffering plague-tormented country.
Indeed I am surprised that no purification was made,
Even without the express command of heaven.
The death of a man so worthy, and your King,
Should surely have been probed to the utmost. Be that as it
        may,
Now that I hold the place that he once held –
His bed, his wife – whose children, had fate so willed,
Would have grown to be another bond of blood between
And upon him, alas, has this disaster fallen;   [us –

I mean to fight for him now, as I would fight
For my own father, and leave no way untried
To bring to light the killer of Laius,
The son of Labdacus, the son of Polydorus, the son of Cad-
    mus, the son of Agenor.
    The gods curse all that disobey this charge!
For them the earth be barren of harvest, for them
Women be childless; and may this present calamity,
And worse than this, pursue them to their death!
For the rest – you sons of Cadmus who are on my side –
May Justice and all the gods be with you for ever.

CHORUS: Under your curse, O King, I make bold to answer:
I am not the man, nor can I point him out.
The question came from Phoebus, and he, if anyone,
Could surely tell us who the offender is.

OEDIPUS: No doubt, but to compel a god to speak
Against his will, is not in mortal power.

CHORUS: I have another thing to say.

OEDIPUS: Say on.
Second, or third, thoughts – we will hear them all.

CHORUS: To the lord Phoebus the lord Teiresias
Stands nearest, I would say, in divination.
He is the one who could help us most in our search.

OEDIPUS: I have not overlooked it. I have sent for him –
It was Creon's advice – twice I have sent for him,
And am much surprised he is not already here.

CHORUS:
There were rumours, of course; but mostly old wives' tales.

OEDIPUS: Rumours? What rumours? I must hear them all.

CHORUS:
He was said to have been killed by travellers on the road.

OEDIPUS: So I have heard. But where are the witnesses?

CHORUS: He'd be a bold man, sir, that would pay no heed
To such a curse as yours, when he had heard it.

OEDIPUS: Will he fear words, that did not shrink from the
    deed?

B

CHORUS:
>   There is one can find him out. They are bringing the prophet
>   In whom, of all men, lives the incarnate truth.
>
>>   *Enter* TEIRESIAS, *blind, led by an attendant.*

OEDIPUS:
>   Teiresias, we know there is nothing beyond your ken;
>   Lore sacred and profane, all heavenly and earthly knowledge
>   Are in your grasp. In your heart, if not with the eye,
>   You see our city's condition: we look to you
>   As our only help and protector. We have sent –
>   They may have told you – to Phoebus, and he has answered
>   The only way of deliverance from our plague
>   Is for us to find out the killers of Laius
>   And kill or banish them.
>   Now, sir, spare not your skill
>   In bird-lore or whatever other arts
>   Of prophecy you profess. It is for yourself,
>   It is for Thebes, it is for me. Come, save us all,
>   Save all that is polluted by this death.
>   We look to you. To help his fellow-men
>   With all his power is man's most noble work.

TEIRESIAS:
>   Wise words; but O, when wisdom brings no profit,
>   To be wise is to suffer. And why did I forget this,
>   Who knew it well? I never should have come.

OEDIPUS: It seems you bring us little encouragement.

TEIRESIAS: Let me go home. It will be easier thus
>   For you to bear your burden, and me mine.

OEDIPUS:
>   Take care, sir. You show yourself no friend to Thebes,
>   Whose son you are, if you refuse to answer.

TEIRESIAS: It is because I see your words, sir, tending
>   To no good end; therefore I guard my own.

OEDIPUS:
>   By the gods! If you know, do not refuse to speak!
>   We all beseech you; we are all your suppliants.

TEIRESIAS: You are all deluded. I refuse to utter
  The heavy secrets of my soul – and yours.
OEDIPUS:
  What? Something you know, and will not tell? You mean
  To fail us and to see your city perish?
TEIRESIAS: I mean to spare you, and myself. Ask me
  No more. It is useless. I will tell you nothing.
OEDIPUS: Nothing? Insolent scoundrel, you would rouse
  A stone to fury! Will you never speak?
  You are determined to be obstinate to the end?
TEIRESIAS: Do not blame me; put your own house in order.
OEDIPUS: Hear him! Such words – such insults to the State
  Would move a saint to anger.
TEIRESIAS: What will be
  Will be, though I should never speak again.
OEDIPUS: What is to be, it is your trade to tell.
TEIRESIAS: I tell no more. Rage with what wrath you will.
OEDIPUS: I shall; and speak my mind unflinchingly.
  I tell you I do believe *you* had a hand
  In plotting, and all but doing, this very act.
  If you had eyes to see with, I would have said
  Your hand, and yours alone, had done it all.
TEIRESIAS: You would so? Then hear this: upon your head
  Is the ban your lips have uttered – from this day forth
  Never to speak to me or any here.
  You are the cursed polluter of this land.
OEDIPUS: You dare to say it! Have you no shame at all?
  And do you expect to escape the consequence?
TEIRESIAS: I have escaped. The truth is my defence.
OEDIPUS: Whose work is this? This is no soothsaying.
TEIRESIAS:
  You taught me. You made me say it against my will.
OEDIPUS: Say it again. Let there be no mistake.
TEIRESIAS:
  Was it not plain? Or will you tempt me further?
OEDIPUS: I would have it beyond all doubt. Say it again.

TEIRESIAS: I say that the killer you are seeking is yourself.

OEDIPUS: The second time. You shall be sorry for this.

TEIRESIAS: Will you have more, to feed your anger?

OEDIPUS: Yes!
  More, and more madness. Tell us all you know.

TEIRESIAS: I know, as you do not, that you are living
  In sinful union with the one you love,
  Living in ignorance of your own undoing.

OEDIPUS:
  Do you think you can say such things with impunity?

TEIRESIAS: I do – if truth has any power to save.

OEDIPUS: It has – but not for you; no, not for you,
  Shameless and brainless, sightless, senseless sot!

TEIRESIAS: You are to be pitied, uttering such taunts
  As all men's mouths must some day cast at *you*.

OEDIPUS: Living in perpetual night, you cannot harm
  Me, nor any man else that sees the light.

TEIRESIAS: No; it is not for me to bring you down.
  That is in Apollo's hands, and he will do it.

OEDIPUS (*scenting a possible connection with Creon's embassy*):
  Creon! Was this trick his, then, if not yours?

TEIRESIAS: Not Creon either. Your enemy is yourself.

OEDIPUS (*pursuing his own thought*):
  Ah, riches and royalty, and wit matched against wit
  In the race of life, must they always be mated with envy?
  Must Creon, so long my friend, my most trusted friend,
  Stalk me by stealth, and study to dispossess me
  Of the power this city has given me – freely given –
  Not of my asking – setting this schemer on me,
  This pedlar of fraudulent magical tricks, with eyes
  Wide open for profit, but blind in prophecy?
(*To* TEIRESIAS) What was your vaunted seercraft ever worth?
  And where were you, when the Dog-faced Witch was here?
  Had you any word of deliverance then for our people?
  There was a riddle too deep for common wits;
  A seer should have answered it; but answer came there none

From you; bird-lore and god-craft all were silent.
Until *I* came – I, ignorant Oedipus, came –
And stopped the riddler's mouth, guessing the truth
By mother-wit, not bird-lore. This is the man
Whom you would dispossess, hoping to stand
Nearest to Creon's throne. You shall repent,
You and your fellow-plotter, of your zeal
For scapegoat-hunting. Were you not as old
As you appear to be, sharp punishment
Would soon convince you of your wickedness.

CHORUS: Sir, to our thinking, both of you have spoken
In the heat of anger. Surely this is not well,
When all our thought should be, how to discharge
The god's command.

TEIRESIAS: King though you are, one right –
To answer – makes us equal; and I claim it.
It is not you, but Loxias, whom I serve;
Nor am I bound to Creon's patronage.
You are pleased to mock my blindness. Have you eyes,
And do not see your own damnation? Eyes,
And cannot see what company you keep?
Whose son are you? I tell you, you have sinned –
And do not know it – against your own on earth
And in the grave. A swift and two-edged sword,
Your mother's and your father's curse, shall sweep you
Out of this land. Those now clear-seeing eyes
Shall then be darkened, then no place be deaf,
No corner of Cithaeron echoless,
To your loud crying, when you learn the truth
Of that sweet marriage-song that hailed you home
To the fair-seeming haven of your hopes –
With more, more misery than you can guess,
To show you what you are, and who they are
That call you father. Rail as you will at Creon,
And at my speaking – you shall be trodden down
With fouler scorn than ever fell on man.

OEDIPUS: Shall I bear more of this? Out of my sight!
  Go! Quickly, go! Back where you came from! Go!
TEIRESIAS: I will. It was your wish brought me here, not mine.
OEDIPUS: Had I known what madness I was to listen to,
  I would have spared myself the trouble.
TEIRESIAS: Mad I may seem
  To you. Your parents would not think me so.
OEDIPUS:
  What's that? My parents? Who then ... gave me birth?
TEIRESIAS:
  This day brings you your birth; and brings you death.
OEDIPUS:
  Man, must you still wrap up your words in riddles?
TEIRESIAS: Were you not famed for skill at solving riddles?
OEDIPUS: You taunt me with the gift that is my greatness?
TEIRESIAS: Your great misfortune, and your ruin.
OEDIPUS: No matter!
  I have saved this land from ruin. I am content.
TEIRESIAS:
  Well, I will go. Your hand, boy. Take me home.
OEDIPUS: We well can spare you. Let him take you home.
TEIRESIAS: When I have said my all. Thus, to your face,
  Fearful of nothing you can do to me:
  The man for whom you have ordered hue and cry,
  The killer of Laius – that man is *here*;
  Passing for an alien, a sojourner here among us;
  But, as presently shall appear, a Theban born,
  To his cost. He that came seeing, blind shall he go;
  Rich now, then a beggar; stick-in-hand, groping his way
  To a land of exile; brother, as it shall be shown,
  And father at once, to the children he cherishes; son,
  And husband, to the woman who bore him; father-killer,
  And father-supplanter.
  Go in, and think on this.
  When you can prove me wrong, then call me blind.
                    Exeunt.

CHORUS:

From the Delphian rock the heavenly voice denounces
The shedder of blood, the doer of deeds unnamed.
Who is the man?
Let him fly with the speed of horses racing the wind.
The son of Zeus, armed with his fires, his lightnings,
Leaps to destroy,
And the Fates sure-footed close around him.

Out from the snowy dawn on high Parnassus
The order flashed, to hunt a man from his hiding.
And where is he?
In forest or cave, a wild ox roaming the mountains,
Footing a friendless way; but the deathless voices
Live in his ear;
From the Heart of Earth they cry against him.

Terrible things indeed has the prophet spoken.
We cannot believe, we cannot deny; all's dark.
We fear, but we cannot see, what is before us.
Was there a quarrel between the house of Labdacus
And the son of Polybus? None that we ever knew,
For which to impugn the name of Oedipus,
Or seek to avenge the house of Labdacus
For the undiscovered death.

All secrets of earth are known to Zeus and Apollo;
But of mortal prophets, that one knows more than another
No man can surely say; wisdom is given
To all in their several degrees. I impute no blame
Till blame is proved. He faced the winged Enchantress,
And stood to the test, winning golden opinions.
Never, therefore, will I consent
To think him other than good.

Enter CREON.

CREON: Citizens! They tell me that King Oedipus
Has laid a slanderous accusation on me.

I will not bear it! If he thinks that I
Have done him any harm, by word or act,
In this calamitous hour, I will not live –
Life is too long a time – to hear such scandal!
Nay, more than scandal, a grievous imputation,
If you, my friends, my country, call me traitor.

CHORUS: The words, I think, were spoken in the stress
Of anger, ill-considered.

CREON: And did he say
The prophet lied under my instigation?

CHORUS: He did; with what intention I cannot tell.

CREON: Said with unflinching eye was it? Deliberate –
This accusation that he made against me?

CHORUS: I do not scrutinize my master's actions.
But here he comes.

Enter OEDIPUS.

OEDIPUS: Well, sir? What brings you here?
Have you the face to stand before my door,
Proved plotter against my life, thief of my crown?
Do you take me for a coward, or a fool?
Did you suppose I wanted eyes to see
The plot preparing, wits to counter it?
And what a foolish plot! You, without backing
Of friends or purse, to go in quest of kingship!
Kingdoms are won by men and moneybags.

CREON: Hear my reply. And when you know, then judge.

OEDIPUS: I doubt your eloquence will teach me much.
You are my bitterest enemy; that I know.

CREON: First, let me tell you –

OEDIPUS: Tell me anything
Except that you are honest.

CREON: Can you believe
This obstinacy does you any good?

OEDIPUS: Can *you* believe that you may carry on
Intrigues against your house and go scot-free?

CREON: I should be a fool to believe it. Tell me, though,

What wrong you think I have done you.

OEDIPUS: Was it you
  That made me bring that canting prophet here?

CREON: It was; and I would do the same again.

OEDIPUS: Tell me ... how long ago did Laius ...

CREON: Did Laius – what? I do not understand.

OEDIPUS: How long is it since Laius ... disappeared?

CREON: A long time now; longer than I can say.

OEDIPUS: Was this old prophet at his business then?

CREON: Yes, held in equal honour then as now.

OEDIPUS: In those days, did he ever mention me?

CREON: Not in my hearing.

OEDIPUS: Was there no inquest made
  Into this death?

CREON: Indeed there was. In vain.

OEDIPUS: And the man of wisdom – why was he silent then?

CREON: I do not presume to say more than I know.

OEDIPUS:
  One thing you know, and would be wise to confess.

CREON: What I know I will freely confess. What do I know?

OEDIPUS:
  This: that without your prompting, the fortune-teller
  Would never have dared to name *me* killer of Laius.

CREON: If he did so, you know best. But give me leave,
  As you have questioned me, to question you.

OEDIPUS: Ask on. You cannot prove me guilty of blood.

CREON: Are you my sister's husband?

OEDIPUS: Sir, I am.

CREON: And she your equal partner in rule and possession?

OEDIPUS: All that she can desire is hers by right.

CREON: Have I a third and equal share of honour?

OEDIPUS: You have; so much the more your proven falseness.

CREON: But I deny it. Reason with yourself,
  As I; and ask, would any man exchange
  A quiet life, with royal rank assured,
  For an uneasy throne? To be a king

In name, was never part of my ambition;
Enough for me to live a kingly life.
What more could any moderate man desire?
I have your ear for all my fair requests;
But, in your place, I should have much to do
That irked me. How could kingship please me more
Than royalty and rule without regret?
I am not yet so besotted as to seek
More honours than are good for me. I stand
In all men's favour, I am all men's friend.
Why, those who seek your audience, ask for me,
Knowing that way the surest to success!
And would I change this life for the other? No;
None but a fool would be so faithless. Treason?
That's not my policy, nor, if I know it,
The policy of any friend of mine.

　　To test me; first, go to the Pythian shrine;
Ask if the message I brought back was true.
Second; prove me guilty of any compact
With the soothsayer; then take me and condemn
To death. My voice will join with yours in the sentence.

　　But charged behind my back on blind suspicion
I will not be. To slur a good man's name
With baseless slander is one crime – another
Is rashly to mistake bad men for good.
Cast out an honest friend, and you cast out
Your life, your dearest treasure. Time will teach
The truth of this; for time alone can prove
The honest man; one day proclaims the sinner.

CHORUS: Good words; and fitting for a prudent man
　　To hear and heed. Quick thoughts are seldom safest.

OEDIPUS: When a quick plotter's on the move, my friend,
　　It's safest to be quick in counter-plotting.
　　Am I to sit and wait for him, and lose
　　My opportunity while he takes his?

CREON: What do you want then? Will you banish me?

OEDIPUS:
  By no means. I would have you dead, not banished.
CREON: If you can show in what way I have wronged you –
OEDIPUS: Still clinging to your obstinate arguments?
CREON: Because I know you are wrong.
OEDIPUS: I know I am right.
CREON: In your *own* eyes, not in mine.
OEDIPUS: *You* are a knave.
CREON: And what if you are mistaken?
OEDIPUS: Kings must rule.
CREON: Not when they rule unjustly.
OEDIPUS: Hear him, Thebes!
  My city!
CREON: Yours? Is she not also mine?
CHORUS: Sirs, sirs, enough. Here comes the queen, Jocasta.
  She should be able to compose this quarrel.
          Enter JOCASTA *from the Palace.*
JOCASTA: What is the meaning of this loud argument,
  You quarrelsome men? I wonder you are not ashamed,
  In this time of distress, to air your private troubles.
  Come in, my husband; and Creon, you go home.
  You are making much of some unimportant grievance.
CREON: Not so, my sister. Your husband Oedipus
  Condemns me out of hand with a terrible sentence,
  A choice of death or banishment.
OEDIPUS: It is true.
  I have found him craftily plotting against my person.
CREON: May the curse of heaven rest on me for ever,
  If I am guilty of any such design!
JOCASTA: For the love of God, believe it, Oedipus!
  For his oath's sake, O believe it, and for mine
  And theirs who are here to witness!
CHORUS: Consent, O King, consent.
  Be merciful, and learn to yield.
OEDIPUS: And why should I repent?
CHORUS: His oath should be his shield.

Who never played you false before.

OEDIPUS: You know for what you pray?

CHORUS: We know.

OEDIPUS: Say more.

CHORUS: He swore
   His friendship; is it right to cast away
   A friend, condemned unheard.
   Upon an idle word?

OEDIPUS: In asking this you ask my death or banishment.

CHORUS: Forbid the thought! O by the Lord of Life,
   The Sun, forbid! Lost may I be
   To God and man, if it was ever mine.
   But while our people pine,
   My heart is racked anew
   If you,
   My princes, add your strife
   To our old misery.

OEDIPUS: Then let him go; even though it mean my death
   Or exile in disgrace. Your voice, not his,
   Has won my mercy; him I hate for ever.

CREON: In mercy obdurate, as harsh in anger –
   Such natures earn self-torture.

OEDIPUS: Will you begone?

CREON: I will; unjustly judged by you alone.

                              Exit

CHORUS: Persuade, madam, persuade
   The King to go awhile apart.

JOCASTA: How was this trouble made?

CHORUS: Wild surmise; and the smart
   Of baseless calumny grew hot.

JOCASTA: Each holding each to blame?

CHORUS: Just so.

JOCASTA: For what?

CHORUS: Ask not
   Again; enough our stricken country's shame.
   To let this other rest

Where it remains, were best.

OEDIPUS:
A fine peacemakers' part your worships would have played!

CHORUS: Hear yet again, O King; believe us true!
Could ours be such simplicity
As rashly from his sheltering arms to stray,
Whose wisdom in the day
Of wrath upheld our land,
Whose hand
Again shall lead us through
Storm to tranquillity?

JOCASTA: Will you not tell me too? Tell me, I implore you,
Why you have conceived this terrible hatred against him.

OEDIPUS: I will. You are more to me than these good men.
The fault is Creon's, and his this plot against me.

JOCASTA: How was it his? What is the accusation?

OEDIPUS: He says the murder of Laius was my doing.

JOCASTA: From his own knowledge, or other men's report?

OEDIPUS: Ah, there's his cleverness; he shields himself
By using a rascally soothsayer as his tool.

JOCASTA: Then absolve yourself at once. For I can tell you,
No man possesses the secret of divination.
And I have proof. An oracle was given to Laius –
From Phoebus, no; but from his ministers –
That he should die by the hands of his own child,
His child and mine. What came of it? Laius,
It is common knowledge, was killed by outland robbers
At a place where three roads meet. As for the child,
It was not yet three days old, when he cast it out
(By other hands, not his) with rivetted ankles
To perish on the empty mountain-side.
There, then, Apollo did not so contrive it.
The offspring did not kill the father; the father,
For all his fears, was killed – not by his son.
Yet such were the prophets' warnings. Why should you,
Then, heed them for a moment? What he intends,

The god will show us in his own good time.

OEDIPUS: My wife, what you have said has troubled me.
My mind goes back ... and something in me moves ...

JOCASTA:
Why? What is the matter? How you turn and start!

OEDIPUS: Did you not say that Laius was killed
At a place where three roads meet?

JOCASTA: That was the story;
And is the story still.

OEDIPUS: Where? In what country?

JOCASTA: The land called Phocis – where the road divides,
Leading to Delphi and to Daulia.

OEDIPUS: How long ago did it happen?

JOCASTA: It became known
A little time before your reign began.

OEDIPUS: O God, what wilt thou do to me!

JOCASTA: Why, Oedipus,
What weighs upon your mind?

OEDIPUS: O do not ask!
But tell me, what was Laius like? How old?

JOCASTA: Tall – silver-frosted hair – about your figure.

OEDIPUS: Ah, wretch! Am I unwittingly self-cursed?

JOCASTA: What, O my King, what is it? You frighten me.

OEDIPUS: Had then the prophet eyes? O is it possible?
To prove it certain, tell me one thing more.

JOCASTA: You frighten me. I will tell you all I know.

OEDIPUS: How was the King attended? By a few,
Or in full state with numerous bodyguard?

JOCASTA: Five men in all, a herald leading them;
One carriage only, in which King Laius rode.

OEDIPUS: Clearer, alas, too clear! Who told you this?

JOCASTA: A servant, the only survivor that returned.

OEDIPUS: Is he still in the household?

JOCASTA: No. When he came back,
And found you king in his late master's place,
He earnestly begged me to let him go away

Into the country to become a shepherd,
Far from the city's eyes. I let him go.
Poor fellow, he might have asked a greater favour;
He was a good slave.

OEDIPUS: Could we have him here
Without delay?

JOCASTA: We could. Why do you ask?

OEDIPUS: O wife, I fear ... I fear that I have said
Too much, and therefore I must see this man.

JOCASTA: Well, you shall see him. Meantime, may I not hear
What weighs so heavily on your heart?

OEDIPUS: You shall.
If things are as I see them, you are the first
To whom I would tell my story. Listen then.
    My father was a Corinthian, Polybus;
My mother a Dorian, Meropé. At home
I rose to be a person of some pre-eminence;
Until a strange thing happened – a curious thing –
Though perhaps I took it to heart more than it deserved.
One day at table, a fellow who had been drinking deeply
Made bold to say I was not my father's son.
That hurt me; but for the time I suffered in silence
As well as I could. Next day I approached my parents
And asked them to tell me the truth. They were bitterly
That anyone should dare to put such a story about;   [angry
And I was relieved. Yet somehow the smart remained;
And a thing like that soon passes from hand to hand.
    So, without my parents' knowledge, I went to Pytho;
But came back disappointed of any answer
To the question I asked, having heard instead a tale
Of horror and misery: how I must marry my mother,
And become the parent of a misbegotten brood,
An offence to all mankind – and kill my father.
At this I fled away, putting the stars
Between me and Corinth, never to see home again,
That no such horror should ever come to pass.

My journey brought me into the neighbourhood where
Your late king met his end. Listen, my wife:
This is the truth.
When I came to the place where three roads join, I met
A herald followed by a horse-drawn carriage, and a man
Seated therein, just as you have described.
The leader roughly ordered me out of the way ;
And his venerable master joined in with a surly command.
It was the driver that thrust me aside, and him I struck,
For I was angry. The old man saw it, leaning from the
        carriage,
Waited until I passed, then, seizing for weapon
The driver's two-pronged goad, struck me on the head.
He paid with interest for his temerity;
Quick as lightning, the staff in this right hand
Did its work; he tumbled headlong out of the carriage,
And every man of them there I killed.
    But now,
If the blood of Laius ran in this stranger's veins,
Is there any more wretched mortal than I, more hated
By God and man? It is I whom no stranger, no citizen,
Must take to his house; I to whom none may speak;
On me is the curse that none but I have laid.
His wife! – these hands that killed him have touched *her*!
Is this my sin? Am I not utterly foul?
Banished from here, and in my banishment
Debarred from home and from my fatherland,
Which I must shun for ever, lest I live
To make my mother my wife, and kill my father ...
My father ... Polybus, to whom I owe my life.
Can it be any but some monstrous god
Of evil that has sent this doom upon me?
    O never, never, holy powers above,
May that day come! May I be sooner dead
And blotted from the face of earth, than live
To bear the scars of such vile circumstance.

CHORUS: Sir, these are terrible words. But yet be hopeful,
Until you learn the whole truth from our witness.

OEDIPUS: That is my only hope; to await the shepherd.

JOCASTA: And why? What help do you expect from him?

OEDIPUS: This: if we find his story fits with yours,
I am absolved.

JOCASTA: In what particular point?
What did I say?

OEDIPUS: You said he spoke of *robbers* –
That *robbers* killed him. If he still says *robbers*,
It was not I; one is not more than one.
But if he speaks of one lone wayfarer,
There is no escape; the finger points to me.

JOCASTA: Oh but I assure you that was what he said;
He cannot go back on it now – the whole town heard it.
Not only I. And even if he changes his story
In some small point, he cannot in any event
Pretend that Laius died as was foretold.
For Loxias said a child of mine should kill him.
It was not to be; poor child, it was he that died.
A fig for divination! After this
I would not cross the road for any of it.

OEDIPUS: You are right. Still, let us have the shepherd here.
Send one to fetch him.

JOCASTA: I will at once. Come in.
I will do nothing other than you wish.

Exeunt.

CHORUS:
I only ask to live, with pure faith keeping
In word and deed that Law which leaps the sky,
Made of no mortal mould, undimmed, unsleeping
Whose living godhead does not age or die.

Pride breeds the Tyrant; swollen with ill-found booty,
From castled height Pride tumbles to the pit,
All footing lost. Zeal, stripped for civic duty,
No law forbids; may God still prosper it.

Who walks his own high-handed way, disdaining
True righteousness and holy ornament;
Who falsely wins, all sacred things profaning;
Shall he escape his doomed pride's punishment?

Shall he by any armour be defended
From God's sharp wrath, who casts out right for wrong?
If wickedness for virtue be commended,
Farewell, sweet harmonies of sacred song;

Farewell, Abaean and Olympian altar;
Farewell, O Heart of Earth, inviolate shrine,
If at this time your omens fail or falter,
And man no longer own your voice divine.

Zeus! If thou livest, all-ruling, all-pervading,
Awake; old oracles are out of mind;
Apollo's name denied, his glory fading;
There is no godliness in all mankind.

Enter JOCASTA *from the Palace, carrying
a garlanded branch and incense.*

JOCASTA: My lords, I am minded to visit the holy temples,
Bringing in my hands these tokens of supplication
And gifts of incense. The King is over-wrought
With fancies, and can no longer sanely judge
The present by the past, listening to every word
That feeds his apprehension. I can do nothing
To comfort him.
To thee, Bright Shining Apollo,
Who art nearest to my door, is my first prayer.
Save us from the curse of this uncleanness, save!
We are afraid, seeing our master-pilot distraught.
She makes her oblations to the altars.

Enter a MESSENGER FROM CORINTH.

MESSENGER: By your leave, strangers; I am seeking the
house of Oedipus.

Can you guide me to it – or to him, if you know where he is?

CHORUS: This is the house, sir; and he is within. This lady
  Is his wife and the mother of his children.

MESSENGER: Blessing attend her,
  And all her house, true consort of such a man.

JOCASTA: Blessing on you, sir, and thanks for your kindly
  You bring a request or message, sir?   [greeting.

MESSENGER: Good news
  For your husband, honourable lady, and for his house.

JOCASTA: What news? And from whom?

MESSENGER: From Corinth. You cannot but be glad
  At the message – though you may also be distressed.

JOCASTA: What is it that can have such power to please and

MESSENGER: [grieve?
  Our people – such was the talk – will make him king
  Of all the Isthmus.

JOCASTA: Is Polybus king no longer?

MESSENGER: King Polybus, madam, is dead and in his grave.

JOCASTA: What? Dead? The father of Oedipus?

MESSENGER: Ay, on my life.

JOCASTA(to an attendant): Girl! To your master quickly!
  Tell him this news. (The attendant goes)
  Where are you now, divine prognostications!
  The man whom Oedipus has avoided all these years,
  Lest he should kill him – dead! By a natural death,
  And by no act of his!

                    Enter OEDIPUS.

OEDIPUS: My dear Jocasta,
  Why have you called me out of doors again?

JOCASTA:
  Hear this man's news; and when you have heard it, say
  What has become of the famous oracles.

OEDIPUS: Who is this man? What news has he for me?

JOCASTA: He comes from Corinth. Your father, Polybus,
  Is dead – dead!

OEDIPUS: What, sir? Tell me yourself.

MESSENGER: I do assure you, sir – if you must have this first –
    He is gone the way of all mortality.

OEDIPUS: By foul play, or the accident of sickness?

MESSENGER: Such little accident as puts the old to sleep.

OEDIPUS: You mean he died of illness, poor old man.

MESSENGER: That, and the tale of years he had fulfilled.

OEDIPUS:

    Well, well ... So, wife, what of the Pythian fire,
    The oracles, the prophesying birds,
    That scream above us? I was to kill my father;
    Now he lies in his grave, and here am I
    Who never touched a weapon ... unless it could be said
    Grief at my absence killed him – and so *I* killed him.
    But no, the letter of the oracle
    Is unfulfilled and lies, like Polybus, dead.

JOCASTA: Have I not said so all this while?

OEDIPUS: You have.
    My fear misled me.

JOCASTA: Think no more of it.

OEDIPUS: There is the other still to fear ... my mother ...

JOCASTA: Fear? What has a man to do with fear?
    Chance rules our lives, and the future is all unknown.
    Best live as best we may, from day to day.
    Nor need this mother-marrying frighten you;
    Many a man has dreamt as much. Such things
    Must be forgotten, if life is to be endured.

OEDIPUS: If she were dead, you might have spoken so
    With justice; but she lives; and while she lives,
    Say what you will, I cannot cease to fear.

JOCASTA: At least your father's death is a relief.

OEDIPUS: Agreed; but while *she* lives, I am not safe.

MESSENGER:

    But pray, sir, who is the woman whom you still fear?

OEDIPUS: Why, sir, Queen Meropé, wife of Polybus.

MESSENGER: And she? How does her life endanger yours?

OEDIPUS: We have an oracle, sir, of deadly tenor.

MESSENGER: Is it one that may rightly be uttered to a stranger?
OEDIPUS: It is. Loxias said I was foredoomed
  To make my mother my wife, and kill my father,
  With my own hands shedding his blood. This is the reason
  Of my long estrangement from Corinth. And I have fared
    well,
  Though nothing can fill the place of absent parents.
MESSENGER:
  Was that the fear that has banished you all this while?
OEDIPUS: Yes. I was determined not to kill my father.
MESSENGER: Then let me rid you of this other fear.
  I came to do you good –
OEDIPUS: My gratitude
  Shall not be stinted.
MESSENGER: And, if the truth were told,
  To do myself good on your coming home.
OEDIPUS: Home, never! Never beneath my parents' roof –
MESSENGER: My dear young man, you are deceived.
OEDIPUS: How so?
  Good sir, for God's sake, tell me.
MESSENGER: This fear that bars you from your home –
OEDIPUS: Ay, that.
  The word of Phoebus may yet be true for me.
MESSENGER: That story of pollution through your parents?
OEDIPUS: Ay, that, sir; that, my ever-present torment.
MESSENGER: All idle, sir; your fears are groundless, vain.
OEDIPUS: How can that be, seeing I am their son?
MESSENGER: No. Polybus is no kin of yours.
OEDIPUS: No kin?
  Polybus not my father?
MESSENGER: No more than I.
OEDIPUS: Come, sir; no more than you? Explain yourself.
MESSENGER: I am not your father, neither is Polybus.
OEDIPUS: How comes it then that I was called his son?
MESSENGER: I will tell you. You were given to him – by me.
OEDIPUS: Given? And yet he loved me as his son?

MESSENGER: He had no other.

OEDIPUS: Was I ... found? Or bought?

MESSENGER: Found, in a wooded hollow of Cithaeron.

OEDIPUS: What brought you there?

MESSENGER: Sheep-tending on the mountain.

OEDIPUS: Were you a hireling shepherd then?

MESSENGER: I was;
  And, by that happy chance, your rescuer.

OEDIPUS: Why, was I in pain or danger when you took me?

MESSENGER: The infirmity in your ankles tells the tale.

OEDIPUS: Oh, that old trouble; need we mention it?

MESSENGER: Your ankles were rivetted, and I set you free.

OEDIPUS: It is true; I have carried the stigma from my cradle.

MESSENGER: To it you owe your present name.

OEDIPUS: O Gods!
  Was this my father's or my mother's doing?

MESSENGER: I cannot say. Ask him who gave you to me.

OEDIPUS: Gave me? Did you not find me, then, yourself?

MESSENGER: Another shepherd entrusted you to my care.

OEDIPUS: And who was he? Can you tell us who he was?

MESSENGER: I think he was said to be one of Laius' men.

OEDIPUS: Laius? Our former king?

MESSENGER: Why, yes; King Laius.
  The man was one of his servants.

OEDIPUS: Is he alive?
  And could I see him?

MESSENGER: Your people here should know.

OEDIPUS: Good men, does any of you know the fellow –
  This shepherd of whom he speaks? Has anyone seen him
  In the pastures or in the city? Speak if you know.
  Now is the chance to get to the bottom of the mystery.

CHORUS: I think he will prove to be that same countryman
  Whom you have already asked to see. The Queen
  Is the one most able to tell you if this is so.

OEDIPUS: My wife, *you* know the man whom we have sent for.
  Is that the man he means?

JOCASTA (*white with terror*): What does it matter
   What man he means? It makes no difference now ...
   Forget what he has told you ... It makes no difference.
OEDIPUS: Nonsense: I must pursue this trail to the end,
   Till I have unravelled the mystery of my birth.
JOCASTA: No! In God's name – if you want to live, this
   Must not go on. Have I not suffered enough?   [quest
OEDIPUS:
   There is nothing to fear. Though I be proved slave-born
   To the third generation, *your* honour is not impugned.
JOCASTA: Yet do not do it. I implore you, do not do it.
OEDIPUS: I must. I cannot leave the truth unknown.
JOCASTA: I know I am right. I am warning you for your
    good.
OEDIPUS: My 'good' has been my bugbear long enough.
JOCASTA: Doomed man! O never live to learn the truth!
OEDIPUS: Go, someone; fetch the shepherd. Leave the lady
   To enjoy her pride of birth.
JOCASTA: O lost and damned!
   This is my last and only word to you
   For ever!

Exit.

CHORUS:
   Why has the Queen, sir, left us in such deep passion?
   I fear some vile catastrophe will out
   From what she dare not tell.
OEDIPUS: Let all come out,
   However vile! However base it be,
   I must unlock the secret of my birth.
   The woman, with more than woman's pride, is shamed
   By my low origin. I am the child of Fortune,
   The giver of good, and I shall not be shamed.
   She is my mother; my sisters are the Seasons;
   My rising and my falling march with theirs.
   Born thus, I ask to be no other man
   Than that I am, and *will know who I am*.

CHORUS: If my prophetic eye fails not, tomorrow's moon
   Makes known to all the earth
   The secret of our master's birth.
   Cithaeron's name shall fill
   Our song; his father, mother, nurse was she,
   And for this boon
   To our great King, praised shall Cithaeron be.
   Phoebus our Lord, be this according to thy will.

     Was this the offspring born of some primeval sprite
   By the love-glance beguiled
   Of mountain-haunting Pan? Or child
   Of Loxias, very son
   To our bright God who walks the high grass-lands?
   Did he delight
   Cyllene's lord? Did Dionysus' hands
   Receive him from a nymph he loved on Helicon?

OEDIPUS: Elders, I think I see our shepherd approaching.
   I guess it is he, though I never set eyes on him.
   He and our Corinthian friend are of like age.
   And those are my men that bring him. It must be he.
   But you could tell more surely, if you know him.
CHORUS: Yes, it is he. I know him. Laius' shepherd –
   As good a man as any in his service.
       Enter an elderly SHEPHERD, *escorted by attendants.*
OEDIPUS: Now, good Corinthian, your evidence first –
   Is this the man you spoke of?
MESSENGER: This is the man.
OEDIPUS: Come now, old shepherd – please to look at me,
   And answer my questions. Were you in Laius' service?
SHEPHERD: Indeed I was, sir; born and bred, not bought.
OEDIPUS: What trade or occupation did you follow?
SHEPHERD: The most part of my life a shepherd, sir.
OEDIPUS: What part of the country did you mostly work?
SHEPHERD:
   'Twould be ... Cithaeron – or somewhere thereabouts.

OEDIPUS: Do you remember having seen this man before?
SHEPHERD:
  What man is that, sir? Where would I have seen him?
OEDIPUS: This man. Did you ever meet him anywhere?
SHEPHERD: I cannot say I did, sir – not to remember.
MESSENGER: I am not surprised. I'll jog his memory.
  He won't forget the days when he and I
  Were neighbours on Cithaeron – he with two flocks
  And I with one; three seasons we were there
  From spring to autumn; and I would drive my flock
  Back Corinth way for winter, and he to Thebes
  To Laius' folds. Was that the way it was?
SHEPHERD: Ay, that's how it was. 'Tis many years ago.
MESSENGER: Well then, maybe you remember a baby boy
  You gave me, and asked me to rear it as my own?
SHEPHERD (*with frightened eyes*):
  What do you mean? What are you asking me to say?
MESSENGER: Why, my old friend, *here* stands your baby boy!
SHEPHERD: Damn you, man, hold your tongue!
OEDIPUS: Come, come, old fellow;
  He speaks more honestly than you, I think.
SHEPHERD: Why, how have I offended, honourable master?
OEDIPUS:
  Not answering straightly his question about that child.
SHEPHERD:
  He doesn't know what he is saying. He is making a mistake.
OEDIPUS:
  If you won't speak willingly, we must make you speak.
SHEPHERD: Don't hurt an old man, sir, for the love of God!
OEDIPUS: Pinion his arms, there!
SHEPHERD: O sir, why, what is this?
  What more do you ask to know?
OEDIPUS: This child he speaks of –
  Was it you that gave it to him?
SHEPHERD: Yes, it was.
  I wish I might have died that very day.

OEDIPUS: As you shall now, unless you tell the truth.

SHEPHERD: 'Twill be my death to tell it.

OEDIPUS: Evasion still!

SHEPHERD: Have I not said I gave it him? What more?

OEDIPUS: Where did it come from? Your home or another's?

SHEPHERD: Not mine. Another man's.

OEDIPUS: What man? What house?

SHEPHERD: By all the gods, master, ask me no more!

OEDIPUS: Answer! If I must speak again, you die!

SHEPHERD: It was ... a child of Laius' house.

OEDIPUS: A slave?
  Or of his own begetting?

SHEPHERD: Must I tell?

OEDIPUS: You must. And I must hear.

SHEPHERD: It was his child,
  They said. Your lady could tell the truth of it.

OEDIPUS: *She* gave it you?

SHEPHERD: Yes, master.

OEDIPUS: To what purpose?

SHEPHERD: To be destroyed.

OEDIPUS: The child she bore!

SHEPHERD: Yes, master.
  They said 'twas on account of some wicked spell.

OEDIPUS: What spell?

SHEPHERD: Saying the child should kill its father.

OEDIPUS: In God's name, what made you give it to this man?

SHEPHERD: I hadn't the heart to destroy it, master. I thought
  'He will take it away to another country, his home'.
  He took it and saved its life – to come to this!
  If you are the man, O then your life is lost!

OEDIPUS: Alas! All out! All known, no more concealment!
  O Light! May I never look on you again,
  Revealed as I am, sinful in my begetting,
  Sinful in marriage, sinful in shedding of blood!
                    Exit.
        The MESSENGER *and* SHEPHERD *depart.*

CHORUS:
All the generations of mortal man add up to nothing!
Show me the man whose happiness was anything more than
    illusion
Followed by disillusion.
Here is the instance, here is Oedipus, here is the reason
Why I will call no mortal creature happy.

With what supreme sureness of aim he winged his quarry;
Grasped every prize, by Zeus! once he had drowned the
The Claw-foot Lady.   [She-devil,
He was our bastion against disaster, our honoured King;
All Thebes was proud of the majesty of his name.

And now, where is a more heart-rending story of
    affliction?
Where a more awful swerve into the arms of torment?
O Oedipus, that proud head!
When the same bosom enfolded the son and the father,
Could not the engendering clay have shouted aloud its
    indignation?

Time sees all; and now he has found you, when you least
    expected it;
Has found you and judged that marriage-mockery, bride-
This is your elegy: [groom-son!
I wish I had never seen you, offspring of Laius,
Yesterday my morning of light, now my night of endless
    darkness!

Enter an ATTENDANT *from the Palace.*

ATTENDANT:
O you most honourable lords of the city of Thebes,
Weep for the things you shall hear, the things you must see,
If you are true sons and loyal to the house of Labdacus.
Not all the waters of Ister, the waters of Phasis,
Can wash this dwelling clean of the foulness within,
Clean of the deliberate acts that soon shall be known,
Of all horrible acts most horrible, wilfully chosen.

CHORUS:

　Already we have wept enough for the things we have
　　known,

The things we have seen. What more will your story add?

ATTENDANT: First, and in brief – Her Majesty is dead.

CHORUS: Alas, poor soul: what brought her to this end?

ATTENDANT: Her own hand did it. You that have not seen,

　And shall not see, this worst, shall suffer the less.

　But I that saw, will remember, and will tell what I re-
　　member

Of her last agony.

　　You saw her cross the threshold

In desperate passion. Straight to her bridal-bed

She hurried, fastening her fingers in her hair.

There in her chamber, the doors flung sharply to,

She cried aloud to Laius long since dead,

Remembering the son she bore long since, the son

By whom the sire was slain, the son to whom

The mother bore yet other children, fruit

Of luckless misbegetting. There she bewailed

The twice confounded issue of her wifehood –

Husband begotten of husband, child of child.

So much we heard. Her death was hidden from us.

Before we could see out her tragedy,

The King broke in with piercing cries, and all

Had eyes only for him. This way and that

He strode among us. 'A sword, a sword!' he cried;

'Where is that wife, no wife of mine – that soil

Where I was sown, and whence I reaped my harvest!'

While thus he raved, some demon guided him –

For none of us dared speak – to where she was.

As if in answer to some leader's call

With wild hallooing cries he hurled himself

Upon the locked doors, bending by main force

The bolts out of their sockets – and stumbled in.

　We saw a knotted pendulum, a noose,

A strangled woman swinging before our eyes.
    The King saw too, and with heart-rending groans
Untied the rope, and laid her on the ground.
But worse was yet to see. Her dress was pinned
With golden brooches, which the King snatched out
And thrust, from full arm's length, into his eyes –
Eyes that should see no longer his shame, his guilt,
No longer see those they should never have seen,
Nor see, unseeing, those he had longed to see,
Henceforth seeing nothing but night ... To this wild tune
He pierced his eyeballs time and time again,
Till bloody tears ran down his beard – not drops
But in full spate a whole cascade descending
In drenching cataracts of scarlet rain.
    Thus two have sinned; and on two heads, not one –
On man and wife – falls mingled punishment.
Their old long happiness of former times
Was happiness earned with justice; but to-day
Calamity, death, ruin, tears, and shame,
All ills that there are names for – all are here.

CHORUS: And he – how is he now? Does he still suffer?

ATTENDANT: He shouts for someone to unbar the doors.
And show all Thebes the father's murderer,
The mother's – shame forbids the unholy word.
Incontinently he will fly the country
To rid his house of the curse of his own lips;
But scarcely has the strength, poor sufferer,
And none to guide him. He cannot bear the pain.
As you shall see. The doors are opening.
Yes, you shall see a sorry spectacle
That loathing cannot choose but pity ...

                Enter OEDIPUS *blind.*

CHORUS: Ah!
Horror beyond all bearing!
Foulest disfigurement
That ever I saw! O cruel,

Insensate agony!
What demon of destiny
With swift assault outstriding
Has ridden you down?
O tortured head!
I dare not see, I am hiding
My eyes, I cannot bear
What most I long to see;
And what I long to hear,
That most I dread.

OEDIPUS: O agony!
Where am I? Is this my voice
That is borne on the air?
What fate has come to me?

CHORUS: Unspeakable to mortal ear,
Too terrible for eyes to see.

OEDIPUS: O dark intolerable inescapable night
That has no day!
Cloud that no air can take away!
O and again
That piercing pain,
Torture in the flesh and in the soul's dark memory.

CHORUS: It must be so; such suffering must needs be borne
Twice; once in the body and once in the soul.

OEDIPUS: Is that my true and ever-faithful friend
Still at my side?
Your hand shall be the blind man's guide.
Are you still near?
That voice I hear
Is yours, although your face I cannot see.

CHORUS:
Those eyes – how could you do what you have done?
What evil power has driven you to this end?

OEDIPUS: Apollo, friends, Apollo
Has laid this agony upon me;
Not by his hand; I did it.

What should I do with eyes
  Where all is ugliness?
CHORUS: It cannot be denied.
OEDIPUS: Where is there any beauty
  For me to see? Where loveliness
  Of sight or sound? Away!
  Lead me quickly away
  Out of this land. I am lost,
  Hated of gods, no man so damned.
CHORUS: Twice-tormented; in the spirit, as in the flesh.
  Would you had never lived to read this riddle.
OEDIPUS: Cursed be the benefactor
  That loosed my feet and gave me life
  For death; a poor exchange.
  Death would have been a boon
  To me and all of mine.
CHORUS: We could have wished it so.
OEDIPUS: Now, shedder of father's blood,
  Husband of mother, is my name;
  Godless and child of shame,
  Begetter of brother-sons;
  What infamy remains
  That is not spoken of Oedipus?
CHORUS: Yet to my thinking this act was ill-advised;
  It would have been better to die than live in blindness.
OEDIPUS: I will not believe that this was not the best
  That could have been done. Teach me no other lesson.
  How could I meet my father beyond the grave
  With seeing eyes; or my unhappy mother,
  Against whom I have committed such heinous sin
  As no mere death could pay for? Could I still love
  To look at my children, begotten as they were begotten?
  Could I want eyes to see that pretty sight?
  To see the towers of Thebes, her holy images,
  Which I, her noblest, most unhappy son
  Have forbidden myself to see – having commanded

All men to cast away the offence, the unclean,
Whom the gods have declared accursed, the son of Laius,
And, having proved myself that branded man,
Could I want sight to face this people's stare?
No! Hearing neither! Had I any way
To dam that channel too, I would not rest
Till I had prisoned up this body of shame
In total blankness. For the mind to dwell
Beyond the reach of pain, were peace indeed.

Cithaeron! Foster-mother! Did you shelter me
For this? Could you not let me die that instant,
Instead of saving me to tell the world
How I was got? Corinth, and Polybus,
My seeming home and parent, did you think
What foul corruption festered under the bloom
Of your adopted son's young loveliness? –
Now found all evil and of evil born.

That silent crossroad in the forest clearing –
That copse beside the place where three roads met,
Whose soil I watered with my father's blood,
My blood – will they remember what they saw,
And what I came that way to Thebes to do?
Incestuous sin! Breeding where I was bred!
Father, brother, and son; bride, wife, and mother;
Confounded in one monstrous matrimony!
All human filthiness in one crime compounded!
Unspeakable acts – I speak no more of them.
Hide me at once, for God's love, hide me away,
Away! Kill me! Drown me in the depths of the sea!
Take me! (*The* CHORUS *shrink from his groping hands*)
For pity, touch me, and take me away!
Touch me, and have no fear. On no man else
But on me alone is the scourge of my punishment.
CHORUS: Creon comes here. On him will now depend,
In act and counsel, the answer to your desires.
He stands our sole protector in your stead.

OEDIPUS: What can I say to him? What plea of mine
   Can now have any justice in his eyes,
   Whom I, as now is seen, have wronged so utterly?
                Enter CREON.
CREON: Oedipus, I am not here to scoff at your fall,
   Nor yet to reproach you for your past misdeeds.
     My friends, remember your respect for the Lord of Life,
   The Sun above us – if not for the children of men.
   The unclean must not remain in the eye of day;
   Nor earth nor air nor water may receive it.
   Take him within; piety at least demands
   That none but kinsmen should hear and see such suffering.
OEDIPUS: I only ask one thing, my gentle friend,
   Whose gentleness to such a one as I am
   Was more than could be hoped for. One thing only –
   For God's love – for your good, not mine –
CREON: What thing,
   So humbly begged?
OEDIPUS: Cast me away this instant
   Out of this land, out of the sight of man.
CREON: Be sure it would have been done without delay,
   But that I await instruction from the god.
OEDIPUS:
   Is not his instruction already plain? The parricide,
   The unclean one, was to die; and here he stands.
CREON: It was so. Yet in the present turn of events
   We need more certain guidance.
OEDIPUS: For my lost life?
   Will you ask the god's direction for one so damned?
CREON: Have you not found good cause to trust him?
OEDIPUS: Yes.
   Then I have only this to ask, of your goodness:
   The funeral rites of her that lies within,
   Provide as you think fit. She is your sister,
   And you will do rightly by her. As for me,
   No longer let my living presence curse
  C

This fatherland of mine, but let me go
And live upon the mountains – and die there.
Cithaeron! Name for ever linked with mine –
On Mount Cithaeron, which my parents chose
To be my deathbed, I will go and die
Obedient to their desires. And yet I know,
Not age, nor sickness, nor any common accident
Can end my life; I was not snatched from death
That once, unless to be preserved
For some more awful destiny. Be it so.
And the children ... Don't trouble yourself about the boys,
Creon; they will be able to fend for themselves
Wherever they go. But the girls, poor little mites,
Have never known a meal without their father;
Everything was shared between us. Take care of them,
    Creon ...
Creon ... If I could touch them once, and weep ...
Once more ...
If you would permit it,
Gracious and generous ...
Just touch them once, and I could think I had them
Once more before my eyes ...

> *The children,* ISMENE *and* ANTIGONE, *have already
> been led in, and stand before* OEDIPUS.

What! Do I hear my darlings sobbing?
Has Creon had pity, and sent them to me?
My darlings,
Are they here?

CREON:

They are here. I had them brought to you. I knew
How much you loved them – how you love them still.

OEDIPUS:

Heaven bless you, Creon, for this, and make your way
Smoother than mine has been.
Where are you, children?
Come, feel your brother's hands. It was their work

That darkened these clear eyes – your father's eyes
As once you knew them, though he never saw
Nor knew what he did when he became your father.
They cannot see you; but they weep with you.
I think of your sorrowful life in the days to come,
When you must face the world: the holy days,
High days and days of state, joyless for you,
Returning sadly home while others play.
And when you look for marriage, will there be men,
Will there be one man brave enough to outface
The scandal that will cling to all my children
And children's children? Is there a name of ill
That is not ours? A father that killed his father;
Despoiled his birth-bed; begetting where he was begot;
Thus they will brand you. Where will you then find
    husbands?
There will be none, my children, for you; your days
Can only end in fruitless maidenhood.
    Menoeceus' son, you are their kinsman still;
You are their only father; we are no more,
Who gave them life. These lost waifs must not wander
Homeless and husbandless; they must not see
Such days as I shall see. Take care of them,
So young, so poor, so lost to all but you.
You will do it? ... Your hand to pledge your promise.
(CREON *gives his hand.*) Friend!
    Children, there is much that you will understand
When you are older; you cannot bear it now.
But in your prayers ask this: that you may live
Not more nor less than well, and so live better
Than did your father.
CREON: This is enough. Will you go in?
OEDIPUS: I must; against my will.
CREON: There is a measure in all things.
OEDIPUS: I have your promise, then?
CREON: What promise?

OEDIPUS: To send me away.

CREON: God will decide, not I.

OEDIPUS: No god will speak for me.

CREON: Then you will have your wish.

OEDIPUS: And your consent?

CREON: I do not speak beyond my knowledge.

OEDIPUS (*satisfied, but reluctantly*): Take me.

CREON: Go then. (OEDIPUS *moves towards the Palace, his arms
  still round the children*) But leave the children.

OEDIPUS: No! Never take them from me!

CREON: Command no more. Obey. Your rule is ended.

  OEDIPUS *is led away*.

CHORUS:

  Sons and daughters of Thebes, behold: this was Oedipus,
  Greatest of men; he held the key to the deepest mysteries;
  Was envied by all his fellow-men for his great prosperity;
  Behold, what a full tide of misfortune swept over his head.
  Then learn that mortal man must always look to his ending,
  And none can be called happy until that day when he carries
  His happiness down to the grave in peace.

  EXEUNT

THE LEGEND CONTINUED

In the play of KING OEDIPUS *it was told how Oedipus uncovered the hideous secret of his unwitting sins. The man whom he had, in an angry moment, slain on the road that lay between Corinth and Thebes was no other than his father Laius; and the wife whom he had married upon his elevation to the throne of Thebes, and who had borne him now two sons and two daughters, was his own mother Jocasta. In his horror at this discovery, and at the self-inflicted death of Jocasta, he destroyed the sight of his own eyes, and, obedient to the curse his own lips had pronounced upon the author of his country's shame and misery, had prayed Creon, now successor to his throne, to banish him for ever from the land. This was promised him; but, in the want of any confirming word from Apollo, the execution of this sentence was long delayed. So Oedipus grew resigned to his humiliation and in some measure comforted by the shelter of his home and the succour of his growing children.*

But, whether upon a revulsion of feeling among his fellow-citizens or by the express command of the god, the order for his banishment was at last pronounced, and Oedipus, now growing old, went forth into perpetual exile. Hereupon discord again rent his family; for while his daughters remained faithful to their father – Antigone, the younger, accompanying him in his wanderings, and Ismene remaining at home to watch for any happier turn of events – his two sons, Eteocles and Polynices, lifted no finger to lighten his burden or stay the execution of his doom. Worse, they rebelled against the regent, Creon; not in alliance together, but in ambitious rivalry for power. While Eteocles secured the suffrages of the greater part of the citizens, Polynices betook himself to Argos, where he married the daughter of King Adrastus and set himself to plan a new onslaught on his fatherland. Meanwhile the blind wanderer and his faithful daughter came in their journeyings to the hamlet of Colonus, within a mile of the city of Athens, over which King Theseus ruled.

But even here his peace was yet to be troubled by the scheming devices of his city and family. For, having banished him, they now found, through the agency of the oracle, that his patronage while alive, and after his death the custody of his remains, were necessary to the accomplishment of their selfish purposes. So the tormented sufferer was not to find rest before he had denounced the feigned repentance of these deceivers and silenced their specious overtures with his last curses.

[Here the play of OEDIPUS AT COLONUS begins]

OEDIPUS AT COLONUS

*

CHARACTERS

Oedipus, *formerly King of Thebes*
Antigone, *his younger daughter*
Ismene, *his elder daughter*
Theseus, *King of Athens*
Creon, *King of Thebes*
Polynices, *son of Oedipus*
A Countryman *of Colonus*
A Messenger
Chorus *of elders of Colonus*
Attendants on Theseus
Attendants on Creon

*

The action of the play takes place in a rustic landscape. The usual central exit from the stage presents the appearance of a rocky path leading by irregular steps to a thickly-wooded grotto. A stone figure, or relief, depicting a rider on a horse, is visible. Exits to right and left lead respectively to the road to Athens, and to the country and sea-coast.

Enter from the country OEDIPUS, *white-haired, blind, and in squalid garments, guided by his daughter* ANTIGONE.

OEDIPUS: Tell me, Antigone – where have you come to now
With your blind old father? What is this place, my child?
Country, or town? Whose turn is it to-day
To offer a little hospitality to the wandering Oedipus?
It's little I ask, and am well content with less.
Three masters – pain, time, and the royalty in the blood –
Have taught me patience. Is there a resting-place,
My child, where I could sit, on common ground
Or in some sacred close? And while I rest,

Ask someone where we are. Strangers like us
Must be taught by the natives and do as they desire.

ANTIGONE: Dear father, I can see towers and a city wall
That seem a long way off. Here, where we are,
There is a kind of sacred precinct, overgrown
With laurel bushes, olive, and wild-vine;
And it is full of the voices of many nightingales.
There is a seat of natural rock. Sit down and rest.
You have come a long way, father.

OEDIPUS: Yes, let me sit.
Lead me, my child. Take care of the blind old man.

ANTIGONE: I should know that lesson by this time, father.

She guides him to a seat within the grove.

OEDIPUS: Now ...
Can you tell me where we have come to?

ANTIGONE: Athens I know,
But am a stranger here.

OEDIPUS: Like everyone we met!

ANTIGONE: Shall I go and ask someone what place it is?

OEDIPUS: Yes, child, if there is anyone dwelling hereabout.

ANTIGONE: Surely there must be. Oh, but I need not go. I
think I see someone approaching now.

OEDIPUS:
Coming this way? Is he coming towards us, Antigone?

ANTIGONE: Yes.

A COUNTRYMAN *of Colonus enters.*
He's here. Speak, father; he is before you now.

OEDIPUS:
Stranger, my daughter, whose eyes are mine and hers,
Tells me there is someone here who can answer our questions.

COUNTRYMAN: Sir, before you ask me any question,
Come from that seat. That place is holy ground.

OEDIPUS: Is it so? To what god is it dedicated, then?

COUNTRYMAN:
It may not be touched, and none may live upon it.
Dread goddesses own it, daughters of Earth and Darkness.

OEDIPUS: What may I call these holy ones in my prayers?
COUNTRYMAN:
As you will; to each the custom of his country;
We call them here the All-seeing Kindly Ones.
OEDIPUS: Then may they be gracious to their suppliant;
For here is the place where I must stay for ever.
COUNTRYMAN: What does this mean?
OEDIPUS: It was fated, and this is the sign.
COUNTRYMAN:
I would not take it upon me to remove you, sir,
Until I have reported to the city for my instructions.
OEDIPUS: At least, good stranger, do not deny me the favour,
Poor wanderer such as I am, to answer my question.
COUNTRYMAN: Ask. I will not refuse you.
OEDIPUS: What is this place?
COUNTRYMAN:
To tell you as much as I know, it is sacred ground,
All this; the great god Poseidon, and the giant Prometheus,
The Lord of Fire, possess it. The spot you stand on
Is called the Brazen Threshold, the Rock of Athens.
This rider is Colonus, known to the country around
As her lord and master, whose name her people bear.
It is not such a place as is famed in song and story,
But its name is great in the hearts of those that live here.
OEDIPUS:
How? Are there people dwelling in this neighbourhood?
COUNTRYMAN:
Surely; their name is the name of their sacred hero.
OEDIPUS: Ruled by one man, or by the general voice?
COUNTRYMAN: The king of the city rules here too.
OEDIPUS: Who is it
That owns this power of counsel and command?
COUNTRYMAN:
His name is Theseus; his father before him was Aegeus.
OEDIPUS:
Could one of your people go as a messenger to him?

COUNTRYMAN:
  To tell him something, or to invite his presence?
OEDIPUS: A little service may win him a great reward.
COUNTRYMAN:
  What kind of reward has a blind man power to give?
OEDIPUS: My words shall not be blind, sir.
COUNTRYMAN: My good friend.
  One can see you are a good man, though in no good plight;
  And I would speak for your good. Stay where you are,
  Where first I saw you, while I go and tell the people –
  Not the city folk, but the dwellers hereabout –
  What I have seen; and they will decide what is best
  Whether you should stay or go away from here.

Exit.

OEDIPUS: Has the stranger gone, my child?
ANTIGONE: He has gone, father. There is no one here but I.
  Say what you like.

Oedipus *prays.*

OEDIPUS: O Holy Ones of awful aspect,
  Whose throne, this seat, was my first resting-place
  In these lands; be gracious to me, be gracious to Apollo,
  Who, with the evil doom he cast upon me,
  Promised me also this rest in the time to come,
  That I should find at last at the seat of the Holy Ones
  Sanctuary, and an end of my tormented days;
  And on them that received me in my sojourning should be
    great blessing,
  With affliction upon them that spurned me and drove me
    out.
  This was the sign he gave that these things should be:
  Earthquake or thunder or the lightning fires of heaven.
  And now I know it is by your certain guidance
  That I have travelled the road to this sacred place.
  No other hand could have led me, at my first coming,
  The sober penitent, to you whom wine delights not,
  Or brought me to this sacred seat of living rock.

Now, therefore, Holy Ones, according to the word of
Grant me, I pray, this fulfilment and close of life,   [Apollo,
If I have found favour, and am not doomed for ever
To groan beneath the heaviest of mortal burdens.
Hear, O gracious daughters of old night!
Hear, O city of Pallas, Queen of cities!
O Athens, have pity on this poor relic of Oedipus,
The shadow, no more the man!

ANTIGONE: Father, enough.
Some elders of the place are coming to look for you,
And see where you have rested.

OEDIPUS: I will be silent.
Yes, hide me, child, hide me from them in the grove
Till we hear what they will say. It will be safest
To know before we act.

They retire into the sacred grove.

Enter the CHORUS *of elders of Colonus, speaking severally as
they search for the intruder.*

CHORUS:
Where? Who is it? Where? He was here.
Where is he hiding?
How dare he?
Look out. Look about.
Look round everywhere.

An old man – some wandering foreigner;
None of us here
Would venture into the sacred close.
The implacable goddesses – Hush!
Take not their name in vain.
Look not, speak not, utter a silent prayer
As you pass.

They told us a trespasser
Was here. Not a sign of him now
Anywhere near the precinct.
Where can he be?

OEDIPUS (*appearing at the entrance of the grove, with* ANTI-
    GONE): I am the man –
  One of those of whom they say,
  Ears are his eyes.
CHORUS: Oh! Sacrilege to see and hear!
OEDIPUS: But I intend no wrong.
CHORUS: Who is he? God defend us!
OEDIPUS: Good elders, I am a man whom none would call
  Well-used by fortune.
  Look, how I make my way by aid of borrowed eyes,
  And lean my strength
  Upon this one weak prop.
CHORUS: Your eyes!
  Were you from birth
  Afflicted so? Long life,
  And sorrowful, is written in your looks.
  I cannot let you stand
  Under this curse. Away!
  You have trespassed, O too far.
  You must not walk in the silent dell,
  There, where the water and the honey-draught are poured.
  Take care, rash visitor; take care!
  O hurry away!
    Does my voice reach you there
  So far? Poor wanderer,
  If you have anything to say,
  Leave the forbidden ground,
  And speak where speech is lawful,
  Or else be silent.
OEDIPUS: What shall we do, my child?
ANTIGONE: We must obey, and do whatever the custom of
    the land requires.
OEDIPUS: Give me your hand.
ANTIGONE: Here, father.
OEDIPUS: Do me no wrong, strangers, if I remove myself
    and put my trust in you.

CHORUS: No one will force you, sir, to quit your resting-
    place against your will.

  OEDIPUS *and* ANTIGONE *move a little way out of the grove.*

OEDIPUS: Further yet?

CHORUS: Further.

OEDIPUS: Again?

CHORUS: Lady, lead him; you understand us.

ANTIGONE: Feel your dark way as I lead you, father.

CHORUS: Stranger on foreign soil,
  Beware, poor wanderer:
  Hate whatsoever we have learned to hate,
  And what we love, revere.

OEDIPUS: Take me, child, to where we may converse with-
    out transgression. We must comply with what is necessary.

    They reach a platform of rock at the edge of the grove.

CHORUS:
  Stay now: you need not come beyond that slab of rock.

OEDIPUS: Here?

CHORUS: It is far enough.

OEDIPUS: I may sit?

CHORUS: To your left, there's a jutting ledge, low down.

ANTIGONE: I'll show you, father. Carefully now –

OEDIPUS: O dear!

ANTIGONE: One step at a time. Lean on my arm.

OEDIPUS: I am so helpless.

    He reaches the seat of rock.

CHORUS: Now you're at ease, poor soul.
  Tell us: who are you, sir?
  Your name, and why you wander in this plight,
  And where your homeland is.

OEDIPUS (*in alarm*): I have no home. You must not –

CHORUS: Must not what?

OEDIPUS: Not ask me who I am – not ask me anything.

CHORUS: But why?

OEDIPUS: So awful an origin –

CHORUS: Say then –

OEDIPUS: O child, what can I say?

CHORUS: Will you not tell us who your father was?

OEDIPUS: O child, child, what shall I do?

ANTIGONE: Tell them, since you have said so much.

OEDIPUS: I must; I cannot hide it.

CHORUS: We're waiting to hear.

OEDIPUS: Maybe you know of one called Laius –

CHORUS (*a gasp of horror*): Ah!

OEDIPUS: And the house of the sons of Labdacus –

CHORUS: O God!

OEDIPUS: And the luckless Oedipus?

CHORUS: You – he?

OEDIPUS: But have no fear –

CHORUS (*a prolonged shout of execration*): Ah ...!

OEDIPUS (*amid the clamour*): My child, my child, what are
    they going to do?

CHORUS: Away! Fly! Begone! Out of our country!

OEDIPUS: You promised – what of your promise?

CHORUS: No one is punished for paying like for like.
    Trick-for-trick is the game now;
    Favours are forfeit. Out you go!
    Quit the country, before you soil it with worse corruption.
    Away! Away!

              ANTIGONE *comes down to plead with them.*

ANTIGONE: Sirs, sirs, you are just and reverent men;
    Though you refuse to hear my poor blind father,
    Because of the things he is known to have done –
    Though they were none of his own devising –
    Yet have some pity for *me*, I beseech you!
    Only for my father's sake I am pleading.
    Let *my* eyes speak for him, mine to yours,
    As it might be a child of your own flesh speaking,
    Asking for pity for one in trouble.

    We have no help but you; you are gods to us.
    We scarce dare hope. Have mercy on us.
    By all you love – wives, children, treasure;

For your God's sake.
God leads us, and no man living
Walks any other way
Than the way God sets before him.

CHORUS: Daughter of Oedipus, we pity you no less than him
For all you suffer; but we fear what the gods may send;
And, fearing, cannot say other than we have said.

OEDIPUS: Ah, then, what help are honour and good name
That end in nothing? There is no help in them.
Is this the reputed godliness of Athens,
City of justice, where, if anywhere,
The suffering stranger should look for refuge and help?
Where are they then for me? You would drive me, would
From my sanctuary, then hound me from your land? [you,
Afraid of my very name? What else? My arm,
My strength? My strength has been in suffering,
Not doing – as you should hear, could I but tell it;
Could tell all that my father and my mother did –
Whence comes, I know, your fear. Was I the sinner?
Repaying wrong for wrong – that was no sin,
Even were it wittingly done, as it was not.
I did not know the way I went. *They* knew;
They, who devised this trap for me, they knew!
    Therefore I beseech you, strangers, by the gods:
You moved me from this place; you must protect me,
Not pay the gods lip-service, only to deny
Their due respect. They look on the godly man
And on the ungodly too. Yes, it is so.
No godless man on earth ever escaped them.
May they be with you, then; and you, forbear,
Forbear to darken the bright star of Athens
By any impious act! I have your pledge.
You accepted my supplication; guard me well.
These ugly scars (*his eyes*) must not forbid your kindness.
I am a holy man, and by holy ordinance
My presence here is to bring this people blessing.

When the King, your master, comes, you shall know all
And understand. Till then, do me no wrong.

CHORUS: Sir, these are solemn words.
We are sensible of the awful import of your pleadings,
And can say no more. The King must be your judge.

OEDIPUS: Yes, where is the ruler of this country, sirs?

CHORUS:
In the city of the land, where his father ruled before him.
That man who found you here and summoned us
Has gone to bring him.

OEDIPUS: And will he come, do you think?
Will he come in person to see a poor blind man?

CHORUS:
To be sure he will, when he has heard your name.

OEDIPUS (*in alarm*):
How will he know it? I did not tell it him.

CHORUS: News travels; there will be rumours on the way,
For it's a goodish step; and when he hears,
He'll come. Your name is known in all the world.
Though he be sleeping, or at his ease, your name
Will bring him fast enough.

OEDIPUS: And may his coming
Bring fulfilment of happiness to his city, as to me!
Goodness must bring its reward, sirs, must it not?

> ANTIGONE *has been looking off into the distance,*
> *and now sees a newcomer approaching.*

ANTIGONE: O Zeus! A miracle! Father, am I dreaming?

OEDIPUS: My child?
What is it?

ANTIGONE: I can see a woman coming this way.
Riding on a colt of Etna; her face is shaded
By a broad Thessalian hat. Is it she? Am I wrong?
Yes ... No ... I can't be sure. Oh what am I thinking of?
It is! It is! She is smiling as she comes.
She is making signs. It is she! My own Ismene!

OEDIPUS: It cannot be.

ANTIGONE:
  Your daughter! My sister! My eyes cannot deceive me,
  And you shall soon believe your ears.
                    Enter ISMENE.
ISMENE: Father!
  And sister! O dearest ones! I have found you at last,
  And now can hardly see you through my tears.
OEDIPUS: My child, is it you?
ISMENE: My poor unhappy father!
OEDIPUS: Are you come at last?
ISMENE: At last, and with what trouble.
OEDIPUS: Touch me, dear child.
ISMENE: A hand for each of you.
OEDIPUS: Sisters together.
ISMENE: O this poor sad life!
OEDIPUS: My life and hers?
ISMENE: And mine; three joined in sorrow.
OEDIPUS: Why did you come, my child?
ISMENE: Thinking of you.
OEDIPUS: With longing?
ISMENE: Yes, and I had things to tell you
  By my own mouth, so had to come alone
  With the only faithful servant that I have.
OEDIPUS:
  Your brothers, where are they in your hour of need?
ISMENE:
  They are – where they are. All is not well with them.
OEDIPUS (*angry*):
  What then? They ape Egyptian manners, do they,
  Where men keep house and do embroidery
  While wives go out to earn the daily bread?
  Instead of troubling themselves about my business,
  They sit at home like girls and let you two
  Bear all the burden of my calamities.
  Antigone here, ever since she grew up
  To womanhood, has been an old man's nurse;

Poor child, the partner of his vagrant life,
Hungry and barefoot, she has roamed the wilds,
Through sun and storm, unflinching, with no thought
For home-keeping, so that her father should not want.
And you, Ismene, have come from time to time
Eluding the people of Thebes, to bring me word
Of any oracle concerning me;
You were my faithful spy, when I was banished.
What is the message now? What errand, Ismene?
You had some purpose; some warning of danger, perhaps?

ISMENE: Father, I will not tell you what trouble I had
To find out where you were and how you lived;
Enough the experience without the telling again.
My message now is about the unhappy story
Of your ill-starred sons.
At first, calmly reflecting
On the old ancestral curse that has held our house
In its deadly grip, they were content that Creon
Should keep the throne, and the city be cleared of stain.
But now, some demon, or the lust of their sinful hearts,
Has filled them with an evil spirit of emulation,
A damnable ambition for power and kingly dominion.
Polynices, the elder, has already been ousted from the throne
By his hot brained brother, and banished from the
    fatherland;
And rumour has it he hides in the vale of Argos,
Contracting a new alliance and gathering about him
A train of armed companions, meaning to fight
Till Argos gloriously triumph over Thebes
Or see her star in the ascendant.
These are not tales, father; this is the truth,
And bitter truth. What mercy the gods will show
On your distress, is more than I can tell.

OEDIPUS: And did you think the gods would yet deliver me?

ISMENE: The present oracles give me that hope.

OEDIPUS: What oracles are they? What prophecy?

ISMENE:
 The people of Thebes shall desire you, for their safety,
 After your death, and even while you live.
OEDIPUS: What good can such as I bring any man?
ISMENE:
 They say it is in you that they must grow to greatness.
OEDIPUS: Am I made man in the hour when I cease to be?
ISMENE: If the gods, who cast you down, now raise you up.
OEDIPUS: A poor return: youth lost, and age rewarded.
ISMENE: Creon will surely come to see to it,
 And it will not be long before he comes.
OEDIPUS: What will he come to do?
ISMENE: To set you close to Theban land, and so
 Possess you, though you may not touch their soil.
OEDIPUS:
 How can I help them, remaining beyond their borders?
ISMENE: If ill befall your grave, it falls on them.
OEDIPUS:
 That could have been guessed without a god's instruction!
ISMENE:
 Well, prompted by this, they seek to have you near them,
 Not leave you to your own devices.
OEDIPUS: So?
 And will they wrap me in their Theban earth?
ISMENE: That cannot be done. Blood-guiltiness forbids it.
OEDIPUS: Then they shall never have me!
ISMENE: Thebes will suffer.
OEDIPUS: In what event?
ISMENE: Under your wrath, when they approach your grave.
                    A pause.
OEDIPUS: Who told you this, my child?
ISMENE: Envoys were sent
 To the Delphian hearth, and brought this message back.
OEDIPUS: Was it indeed of me the god thus spoke?
ISMENE: That was their message.
OEDIPUS: Do my sons know this?

ISMENE: Both know it; and well they understand its purport.
OEDIPUS:
   Villains, then they would rather have their kingdom
   Than have their father back!
ISMENE: Alas, it is true.
OEDIPUS: Then may no god assuage the bitterness
   Of their predestined battle! The bloody warfare
   They have in hand, were I the arbiter,
   I would so end that neither he should stay
   Who now holds power, nor he that was expelled
   Ever return. I was their father, banished
   With ignominy from my fatherland,
   And they did nothing to rescue or defend me;
   Heard me cried outlaw, exiled, and did nothing.
   You say I wished it so, and it was right
   The city should grant my wish? It was not so.
   I wished for death that day; I longed for death
   That day when my soul was on fire, I asked for stones
   To cover me; none gave me my desire.
   Time passed, and the pain abated, and I knew
   How much my wrath had overleaped itself
   To punish me too heavily for my sins.
   Then, then, so late, my city banished me
   By forced expulsion. And *they*, who could have helped me
   As sons should help their father, they did nothing.
   For want of a little word, I went an outcast
   To end my days in misery.
      Only these two, my daughters, have done all
   That women could, to give me what I need,
   Food, and safe conduct, and their loving care.
   Their brothers sold their father for a throne,
   Preferred the sceptre and the kingly power.
   I shall not help them; nothing good will come
   Of *their* ruling over Thebes; of that I am sure
   When I hear these oracles my daughter tells me of,
   And remember those I have known of old, which Phoebus

Has brought at last to their fulfilment here.
  So let them send Creon to look for me,
Or any other mighty man of Thebes!
If you, my friends, will stand beside me now,
With those stern goddesses that live among you,
Your land shall win a great deliverer,
And punishment shall strike my enemies down.

CHORUS:
  We are very sorry for you, Oedipus, and for your
    daughters;
  Moreover your claim to be a source of strength to our land
  Persuades me now to advise you for your good.

OEDIPUS: Dear friend,
  Stand by me and I will do all that you advise.

CHORUS: Then make amends at once to the divinities
  On whose ground you trespassed at your first coming here.

OEDIPUS: Instruct me. What are the rites that I must use?

CHORUS: Bring holy water from where a fresh spring flows;
  In clean hands bring it.

OEDIPUS: A pure libation. Then?

CHORUS: There are vessels there, of delicate workmanship.
  Cover their brims and handles on either side –

OEDIPUS: With sprigs of leaf, or woollen stuffs, maybe?

CHORUS:
  With lamb's wool newly shorn that will be given you.

OEDIPUS: I understand. And then to complete the rite?

CHORUS: Pour the drink-offering, your face towards the
    dawn.

OEDIPUS: From the vessels you spoke of?

CHORUS: Ay, in three libations,
  Of which only the last you empty wholly.

OEDIPUS: What will this last contain?

CHORUS: Water and honey.
  No wine is to be added.

OEDIPUS: I understand.
  The sunless earth will drink it up. And then?

CHORUS: With both hands thrice nine sprays of olive lay,
  While you thus pray.
OEDIPUS: The prayer – ay, this I must mark.
CHORUS: Pray you – or any other on your behalf –
  That these whom we have called the Kindly Ones
  Will kindly look upon their suppliant,
  Who is a saviour too. Pray softly thus,
  Not lifting up your voice; then turn, and go.
  This done, I will defend you without fear;
  Undone, I have no hope for you.
OEDIPUS: My children,
  You hear the advice of those who know this place?
ANTIGONE:
  We have heard it, father. What would you have us do?
OEDIPUS: I cannot go; I am not strong enough,
  And blindness makes me helpless. One of you
  Must go and act for me. In such a service
  One soul, sincere in faith, may stand for thousands.
  Go, one of you, quickly; the other stay with me.
  I cannot move hand or foot without a helper.
ISMENE: I'll do what is required. But I must know
  Where the place is.
CHORUS: Beyond the coppice, lady.
  An attendant there will show you all you need.
ISMENE: I'll go. Look after our father here, Antigone.
  We cannot grudge our pains when parents need us.
                    ISMENE *goes into the grove.*
CHORUS: Cruel it is to awake long-sleeping sorrow;
  Yet I would ask –
OEDIPUS: What now?
CHORUS: Of that affliction to which you were apprenticed,
  That seemed past mending.
OEDIPUS: Kind hosts, do not pry
  Into the infamous things then done to me.
CHORUS: We ask to know the truth
  Of what is, to this day, so widely bruited.

OEDIPUS: O shame!

CHORUS: Be patient, I entreat you –

OEDIPUS: Too horrible!

CHORUS: – as we have granted your requests.

OEDIPUS: I tell you, then, I have endured
　　Foulest injustice; I have endured
　　Wrong undeserved; God knows
　　Nothing was of my choosing.

CHORUS: And the event?

OEDIPUS: Shamefully wedded – tied for my city's sake
　　To a marriage of infamy, unbeknown!

CHORUS: Your mother, as is said,
　　The partner in this bond of shame?

OEDIPUS: To hear it uttered is a death to me. And more –
　　These two – are mine –

CHORUS: No!

OEDIPUS: Children, and curse-bearers –

CHORUS: O God!

OEDIPUS: And fruit of the same mother's womb.

CHORUS: Your daughters and your ...?

OEDIPUS: Sisters! Ay, their father's sisters!

CHORUS: Horror!

OEDIPUS: Horror, and horror recoiling a thousand times
　　Upon my head.

CHORUS: A fate –

OEDIPUS: A fate appalling.

CHORUS: What you did –

OEDIPUS: No doing of mine.

CHORUS: How so?

OEDIPUS: A gift – it was my city's gift,
　　A prize for what I did for her!
　　Would I had never earned it,
　　To be so cursed!

CHORUS: And more – unluckier yet –
　　Did you not kill –

OEDIPUS: What more? What more do you ask?

CHORUS: Your father?

OEDIPUS: Must you strike again? More agony?

CHORUS: You killed him?

OEDIPUS: *Yes*, with justice.

CHORUS: Justice?

OEDIPUS: Yes. You shall hear.
    He whom I killed
    Had sought to kill me first. The law
    Acquits me, innocent, as ignorant,
    Of what I did.

A watcher now descries the approach of THESEUS *and his train.*

CHORUS:
    He is coming! King Theseus, Aegeus' son, comes here.
    He has heard your request and comes to do you service.
        Enter THESEUS. *He stands before* OEDIPUS, *recognising*
                him with grave respect.

THESEUS: The son of Laius. Yes. From all I have heard,
    Long since and often, about the bloody act
    That closed your eyes, you are no stranger to me.
    And what they told me on my way assures me
    That you are really he. The wounded face,
    The pitiful dress, confirm it.
    Then, sad Oedipus,
    Compassion bids me ask you with what suit
    To Athens or to me you here present yourself
    With your companion in distress. Speak freely.
    There is no circumstance that you can tell
    So lamentable that I should shut my ears to it.
    I do not forget my own upbringing in exile,
    Like yours, and how many times I battled, alone,
    With dangers to my life, in foreign lands.
    I could not turn from any fellow-man,
    Coming as you come, or deny him help.
    I know that I am man; in the day to come
    My portion will be as yours, no more, no less.

OEDIPUS: Theseus, your noble kindness in these short words
    Permits as brief an answer. Who I am,
    Whence born, from what land come, you know and have
    It remains to tell my errand, and all is told.   [said.

THESEUS: Then tell me that.

OEDIPUS: I come to offer you
    A gift – my tortured body – a sorry sight;
    But there is value in it more than beauty.

THESEUS: What value?

OEDIPUS: Later you shall know, not now.

THESEUS: When will this gift be known for what it is?

OEDIPUS: When I am dead, and you have buried me.

THESEUS: You only ask for that last office, then,
    Forgetting what comes between, or caring not?

OEDIPUS: Yes; having that, I shall have all my wish.

THESEUS: It is little to ask.

OEDIPUS: It is; but not so little
    The issue – not so little – make no mistake.

THESEUS: You mean, between your sons and me?

OEDIPUS: Ay, that, sir.
    They mean to take me back to Thebes.

THESEUS: Why then,
    If you wished it so, that would be better than exile.

OEDIPUS:
    No, no! When I wished it, they refused to hear me.

THESEUS:
    In a plight such as yours, it is foolish to cherish resentment.

OEDIPUS: Hear me, and then reprove. Have patience, sir.

THESEUS:
    Speak on. I should not judge without full knowledge.

OEDIPUS: Theseus, I have been wronged again and again.

THESEUS: The old, old story of your lineage?

OEDIPUS (impatient): No!
    All *that* is common property.

THESEUS: What, then,
    To mark you as the world's most ill-used man?

OEDIPUS:
   This: driven from home by my own flesh and blood –
   My sons – *my* crime against *my* father bars me
   From hope of restoration.

THESEUS: If that is so,
   Why should they fetch you, if you still remain
   Outlawed, condemned for ever to live apart?

OEDIPUS: The oracle will compel them.

THESEUS: By what sanction?

OEDIPUS: They are threatened with punishment on this very

THESEUS: [land.
   Here? Why? What trouble should ever come between
   My land and theirs?

OEDIPUS: Time, Time, my friend,
   Makes havoc everywhere; he is invincible.
   Only the gods have ageless and deathless life;
   All else must perish. The sap of earth dries up,
   Flesh dies, and while faith withers falsehood blooms.
   The spirit is not constant from friend to friend,
   From city to city; it changes, soon or late;
   Joy turns to sorrow, and turns again to joy.
   Between you and Thebes the sky is fair; but Time
   Has many and many a night and day to run
   On his uncounted course; in one of these
   Some little rift will come, and the sword's point
   Will make short work of this day's harmony.
   Then my cold body in its secret sleep
   Shall drink hot blood. If this is not to be,
   Zeus is not Zeus, and Phoebus is not true!
     But enough: there are things I must not tell of now.
   Ask me no more, but make your own pledge good.
   Be sure you cannot fail of your reward
   In giving Oedipus this dwelling-place,
   Unless heaven means to play him false again.

        THESEUS *turns to confer with the* CHORUS.

CHORUS: This, or to this effect, sir, has been his promise

From the first, and it seems he means to make it good.
THESEUS:
  The kindly intention of such a man must be respected.
  Not only on the ground of mutual hospitality
  To a friend and ally, but also for the goddesses' sake
  Whose suppliant he is, and the boon he will bring to us.
  Such claims compel me to accept his overture
  And house him within our city. While he stays here,
  I appoint you his protector, or if he choose
  To come with me – (*turning to* OEDIPUS) Oedipus, the
  It shall be as you wish.   [choice is yours.
OEDIPUS: May God reward you, sir.
THESEUS: Then will you come with me?
OEDIPUS: If it were lawful –
  But *this* is the place –
THESEUS: This? What have you yet to do?
  Not that I shall forbid you anything.
OEDIPUS: Here I must vanquish those who cast me out.
THESEUS: Is *that* the boon your presence was to bring?
OEDIPUS: It follows, if you perform your promise truly.
THESEUS: You can be sure of that. I'll not betray you.
OEDIPUS: I know you are good. I need not swear you to it.
THESEUS:
  I have given my word; no oath could bind me more.
OEDIPUS (*in new anxiety, perceiving that* THESEUS *means to
      leave him*): What will you do, then?
THESEUS: Why, are you afraid?
OEDIPUS: They will come for me –
THESEUS: These friends will see to that.
OEDIPUS: But – you will leave me?
THESEUS: I know what I must do.
OEDIPUS: Forgive me; I fear –
THESEUS: I see no cause for fear.
OEDIPUS: They have threatened – you do not know –
THESEUS: I know one thing.
  No one shall take you away without my leave.

Threats? What of them? Many an idle threat
Breaks out in the heat of anger, and comes to nothing
When reason takes control. These people of yours
May have been mighty bold in giving out
How they will fetch you away. I think they'll find
A long and stormy passage waiting for them.
You need not fear: apart from my protection
You are in Phoebus' hands. Besides, my name,
Even in my absence, will keep you safe from harm.

Exit.

CHORUS:

Here in our white Colonus, stranger guest,
Of all earth's lovely lands the loveliest,
Fine horses breed, and leaf-enfolded vales
Are thronged with sweetly-singing nightingales,
Screened in deep arbours, ivy, dark as wine,
And tangled bowers of berry-clustered vine;
To whose dark avenues and windless courts
The Grape-god with his nursing-nymphs resorts.

Here, chosen crown of goddesses, the fair
Narcissus blooms, bathing his lustrous hair
In dews of morning; golden crocus gleams
Along Cephisus' slow meandering streams,
Whose fountains never fail; day after day
His limpid waters wander on their way
To fill with ripeness of abundant birth
The swelling bosom of our buxom earth.

Here Aphrodite rides with golden reins;
The Muses here consort; and on these plains,
A glory greater than the Dorian land
Of Pelops owns, or Asiatic strand,
Our sweet grey foster-nurse, the olive, grows
Self-born, immortal, unafraid of foes;
Young knaves and old her ageless strength defies
Whom Zeus and Pallas guard with sleepless eyes.

And last, our Mother-city's chiefest pride
I yet must praise, all other gifts beside,
Poseidon's gift, which makes her still to be
Mistress of horses, mistress of the sea.
Here in these lanes wild horses first obeyed
The bit and bridle; here the smooth oar-blade
In slim and handy shape first learned to leap
And chase the fifty sea-maids through the deep.

ANTIGONE *now sees a newcomer approaching.*

ANTIGONE: Now is the time for this land of happy fame
To match those praises in act!

OEDIPUS: What now, my child?

ANTIGONE: Creon is coming, heavily escorted.

OEDIPUS:
Good elders, let this be my hour of final deliverance!

CHORUS:
It shall be so. We are old, but our country's strength
Is young and lusty still.

Enter CREON, *with attendants; an older man than* OEDIPUS, *but more active, though with less innate authority. The* CHORUS *brace themselves for the challenge, and* CREON *is checked for a moment, but then speaks appeasingly.*

CREON: Gentlemen of Colonus,
Your looks betray a sudden alarm at my coming.
You need not be afraid, nor treat me with violent abuse.
Mine is no violent purpose; I am too old,
And am well aware that the city to which I have come
Is a power in Hellas second to none. I am sent,
Old as I am, to use my influence
To persuade this man to return to Theban land.
I am not any single man's emissary,
But bear this charge from our whole community;
Rightly, since I, as this man's next of kin,
Have borne the brunt of our anguish on his behalf.
    Now Oedipus, poor unhappy man, come home;

Do not refuse me; all your people ask you,
And with good cause; so, more than all, do I.
Unless I am the veriest villain that ever breathed,
I must be sorry for the sorrows of your old age,
Seeing you cast adrift like this, a vagabond,
A beggar, with a sole companion at your side.
Poor child! Could I ever have believed she would come to
So young, condemned to endless tutelage   [this,
Of that sad ruined head, wasting her maidenhood
In cheerless poverty; and so ill-protected
Against any rude assault.
We are all to blame;
We are all accused – you, I, and all our family;
And here in the eye of day it cannot be hid.
O Oedipus! Now by the gods of our fathers, hear me!
Cover our shame; come home to your fathers' city,
Your fathers' house, taking a kindly leave
Of this kind land – she has served you well; but home,
Where you were bred, first claims your piety.

OEDIPUS: Devil! There is no specious argument
You cannot twist to your cunning purposes!
Do you hope to entrap me a second time in the snare
That will drag me to utmost misery? There was a time
When the havoc my hand had wrought so sickened me
That banishment was my dearest wish. I asked it;
You would not grant it. But when my passion was spent,
And home held comfort for me, *then* you were pleased
To hound me out to exile. Little you cared
For kinship and family *then*! Once more you come,
And, seeing me kindly welcomed in this land
By all her people, try to drag me back,
Covering your hate with a cloak of seeming affection.
     Unwanted favours earn no gratitude!
If one refused you everything you asked,
Denied your fondest wish, and then, forsooth,
When you had all your heart's desire, turned round

And gave you charity – would you thank him for it?
Such are your specious gifts – no good at all.
    Let all these men take note of your foul purpose!
You come for me – not to conduct me home,
But to instal me on your frontier,
To save your city from falling out with Athens.
You shall not have your wish! *This* you shall have:
My everlasting curse upon your country!
As for my sons, their heritage in my land
Shall be no larger than the ground they die on.
    Do you not think I read the state of Thebes
With clearer eyes than yours? Surely, and why?
I have more certain guidance, the true word
Of Phoebus and his almighty father, Zeus.
You come here with your artful politic tongue
Primed for sharp practice; but your eloquence, sir,
You'll find, will win you far more harm than good.
But there – you don't believe me. Go your way,
And I'll go mine; hard as it is, I choose it,
And I could be content.

CREON:
    Well? Do you think your verdict in this argument
    Does me more harm than the harm you do yourself?

OEDIPUS: I am satisfied, so long as you gain no ground
    With me or with my friends.

CREON: I am sorry for you.
    Your years have not yet taught you sense, I see;
    A disgrace to your generation still!

OEDIPUS: Wag on,
    Smart tongue! I never knew an honest man
    Subtle in argument.

CREON: True, the ready talker
    May talk much nonsense.

OEDIPUS: Meaning yourself as a pattern
    Of pertinent brevity?

CREON: Not to *your* way of thinking.

OEDIPUS:

  Leave us! These are my friends and I speak for them.
  Call off your spies and jailers, and let me be.
  Here is my home and here I am to stay.

CREON:

  I have done with you! And I call these men to witness –
  I wished you well; you answer me with cursing.
  But when I get you –

OEDIPUS: That will never be.
  I have my allies.

CREON: Well, there are other ways.

OEDIPUS:

  A threat? What does that mean? What have you done?

CREON: Your daughters: one we have already caught
  And taken away; the other will follow shortly.

OEDIPUS: No, no!

CREON: Yes; you'll have more to weep for presently.

OEDIPUS: You have taken my daughter?

CREON: And mean to have the other.

OEDIPUS: Friends, help! You won't betray me! Drive him out!
  Drive this foul devil from your soil!

CHORUS: Away,
  Away, sir! You have done wrong enough.

CREON (*to his men*):
  Arrest her. Force her if she will not come (*they seize her*).

ANTIGONE: O help! O help me, gods and men!

CHORUS: Stop, sir!

CREON: The *man* is yours; but *she* is mine.

OEDIPUS: O sirs!

CHORUS: You have no right –

CREON: I have.

CHORUS: What right?

CREON: She's mine (*he lays hands on her*).

OEDIPUS: O Athens!

CHORUS: Stop, sir! Let her go!
  Or you and I must fight.

CREON: Come if you dare.

CHORUS: We do
　If you persist.

CREON: It's war between our cities if you touch me.

OEDIPUS: As I foretold you.

CHORUS: Let the woman go.

CREON:
　I take no orders; you have no power against me.

CHORUS: Let go, I say!

CREON: *I* say, away with you,
　And look to your own business!

CHORUS: Help! People! Help!
　Our home is in danger! Help!
　Our country attacked!
　Help and defend us!

ANTIGONE: Don't let them take me away!

OEDIPUS: My child, where are you?

ANTIGONE: They're taking me away!

OEDIPUS: Give me your hand.

ANTIGONE: I can't!

CREON: Off with her!

OEDIPUS: Oh, I cannot bear it! Oh!

　　　　　The guards carry ANTIGONE *away.*

CREON: So much for those two props of your infirmity –
　Henceforth you walk without them. As for your wish
　To flout your friends and fatherland, whose orders
　I am here obeying, though I am their king,
　You win: but in time you cannot fail to learn
　That this same angry temper which besets you,
　This spite against your friends, has been your ruin
　Always, as it is now.

He turns to go, but the CHORUS *are now intercepting his retreat,*
　　　　though still not daring to assault him bodily.

CHORUS: Stand fast!

CREON: Hands off!

CHORUS: Not while you hold those women captive.

　D

CREON: So?

    Then I must take another hostage home.
> *He advances upon* OEDIPUS, *now once more*
> *in the sanctuary of the grove.*

CHORUS: What will you do?

CREON: Here is my prisoner.

CHORUS: You could not!

CREON:

    Could – and will. Who will prevent me? Your king?

OEDIPUS: You dare not touch me! Blasphemous beast!

CREON: Be silent!

OEDIPUS: No! By your leave, divinities,
    My curse must yet be spoken. Heartless fiend!
    My eyes were dark long since, and you have torn
    My last poor light, my helpless darling, from me.
    Then may the Sun, the eye of God, reward you,
    And all your issue, with like impotence
    And darken all your days until you die!

CREON: You see, Colonians?

OEDIPUS: They see us both, and judge,
    Knowing that I, who am so ill-used in act,
    Have no defence but cursing.

CREON: I'll hear no more.
    Old and alone, I'll take you.

OEDIPUS: O help!

CHORUS: Stop, sir! You are too bold.
    You cannot do this thing.

CREON: I will.

CHORUS: Then there is law
    No more in Athens.

CREON: Law arms the weaker, when the cause is just.

OEDIPUS: Hear his wild boast!

CHORUS: He shall not make it good,
    God knows.

CREON: God surely knows what you do not.

CHORUS: Sacrilege!

CREON: Sacrilege – if you think so,
Then you must bear it.

CHORUS: Help! Masters and people!
Quick to the rescue! Help!
We are robbed and plundered,
Look to the road there!

Enter THESEUS *with his attendants.*

THESEUS: What's this alarm? What's happening? I heard
your shouts of terror
At the altar of sacrifice, where I was performing my solemn
service
To the God of the Sea, this country's patron, and broke off
To return, with more speed than comfort; tell me all that
has happened.

OEDIPUS:
That voice! My friend – this man is doing me wrong.

THESEUS: What man? And how?

OEDIPUS: Creon – do you not see him? –
Has torn my children from me – my only two.

THESEUS: Truly?

OEDIPUS: As truly as I tell it you.

THESEUS (*to his men*): One of you, quick, to the altars! Tell
everyone to leave the sacrifice and post on horse and
foot to where the hill-road forks. If they don't intercept
the women and their captors there, I'm beaten, and this
foreigner has the laugh on me. Away! (*one goes*)
Yet if I dealt with him as anger prompts me,
And as he well deserves, he'd not escape
Hard usage. In any case, we'll bring him to book
By the law he has brought with him.
(*To* CREON)
Here you stay
Until you cause these women to be brought
Into our sight. You have insulted me,
Disgraced your breed and country. Ours is a land
That lives by justice, knows no rule but law;

And here you blunder in and lay rough hands
On any prize you fancy, snapping your fingers
At our established order. It seems you think
We are a city of slaves, or city of emptiness,
And I a thing beneath your notice! Well,
It was not Thebes that taught you this behaviour;
Her sons are mostly gentlemen. She'd blush
For your assault on me – assault on the gods,
Arresting their defenceless suppliants.
You would not find me coming to your land,
On any pretext, however plausible,
And seizing this or that, without the leave
Of anyone who held authority there.
I'd know my place as a foreigner better than that.
    You're bringing shame upon an innocent city,
Your own; it's evident your lengthening days
Have given you age and robbed you of discretion.
As I have said, I say again: the women
Must be restored without delay, or else
We shall constrain you to remain our guest.
And what I say, I mean.

CHORUS: Now, foreigner,
    You see your error. Coming whence you come,
    You should be honest, but your acts disprove it.

CREON:
    You are wrong, King Theseus. I did not undervalue
    The manhood of Athens, nor the wit of her counsellors,
    When I acted thus. But neither did I expect
    Your people to show such affection for one of my blood
    As to harbour him in defiance of me. I felt certain
    They would never receive a polluted parricide,
    A party to an incestuous union – mother and son.
    I knew the infallible wisdom of the Hill of Ares
    Does not allow asylum to such vagabonds.
    Therefore I felt entitled to claim my prize.
    Even so, I might have spared him, had he not chosen

To hurl foul curses at me and all my race;
For which I thought it fit to take reprisal.
I may be old, but anger does not cool
Except with death – that ends all bitterness.
　　Do what you will, then. I am alone and powerless,
However just my cause. But, whatever you do,
I'm not so old but I'll find some answer to it!

OEDIPUS: Still unrepentant! Is it my grey head
Or yours that is more insulted by such talk –
A stream of vile abuse – of murder and incest
And all the events that have thrust themselves upon me?
The gods so willed it – doubtless an ancient grudge
Against our house. *My* life was innocent,
Search as you will, of any guilty secret
For which this error could have been the punishment,
This sin that damned myself and all my blood.
　　Or tell me: if my father was foredoomed
By the voice of heaven to die by his own son's hand,
How can you justly cast it against *me*,
Who was still unborn when that decree was spoken?
Unborn? Nay, unbegotten, unconceived.
And if, being born, as I was, for this calamity,
I chanced to meet my father and to kill him,
Not knowing who he was or what I did –
How can you hold the unwitting act against me?
Likewise my mother – O shame, that you should force me
To speak as I must about your sister's marriage –
But you have broken all bounds of piety,
And I cannot be silent. She was my mother –
My mother, and knew not – neither of us knew
The thing we did – her shame! – she bore my children.
　　I know, I know it is you that take delight
In slandering her and me. To speak of it
Is as much against my will as was the doing.
Yet this I must say again! I am not condemned,
And shall not be, either for my marrying

Or for my father's murder, which your spite
Persists in casting in my teeth.

    Answer me this one thing: if here and now
Someone came up and threatened to take your life,
Your innocent life, would you then pause to ask
If he were your father – or deal with him out of hand?
I'm sure, as you love life, you'd pay the assailant
In his own coin, not look for legal warrant.
Such, by the gods' contrivance, was my case.
My father himself, if he could live again,
Would not deny it. But you, who know no law,
No scruple in speaking of things unspeakable,
Shout your vile taunts at me in these men's presence.

    At the name of Theseus you are pleased to cringe
And eulogize the ordered state of Athens.
Do you reflect, this land you praise so highly
Pays high respect – above all other lands –
To the holy gods? Yet it was here you tried
To steal an aged suppliant from their sanctuary,
And have already carried off my daughters.
For which affront I call upon these goddesses
With most importunate prayers and supplication
To send me help and defence, that you may learn
What manner of men uphold this city's honour.

CHORUS (*to* THESEUS):
    Our guest is innocent, sir, though cursed by fortune.
    We cannot withhold our aid.

THESEUS: Enough has been said.
    While we stand here, the rogues are on the move.

CREON: What can I do, then, powerless as I am?

THESEUS: Lead on, while I escort you. If the women
    Are still in reach, you shall conduct me to them.
    If the quarry has gone away, we save our pains;
    There are others already on the trail; they'll see to it
    That none of yours gets home to thank his gods.
    Lead on! The biter's bit, the hunter hunted.

What's wrongly got is soonest lost. I warn you,
If you had helpers, as I know you had –
You would not have ventured on this daring outrage
Without some trusty backers – you have lost them;
I'll take good care of that. We'll not have Athens
At anyone's mercy. I think you understand me,
Unless my warnings mean no more to you
Than those you heard when you were at this business.

CREON: I need not quarrel with you here; at home
I shall know what to do.

THESEUS: Threaten as you will,
But march! You, Oedipus, stay here in peace.
I promise you I'll bring your children back,
Or die beside them.

Exit, with CREON.

OEDIPUS: Good Theseus, for your faithful care of me
Good luck be with you.

CHORUS: Who would not wish to be
There when the enemy
Turns to give battle with singing of sword and spear?
That were a sight to see.
Do they draw near
Now to the Pythian shrine,
Now to the hallowed sand
Where the bright torches shine,
Where at the breast of Earth's Mother her votaries
Seek holy mysteries
Locked in gold silence
Under the seal of the singers
Of sweet melody?

    Great Theseus is there
In the thick of the fray;
With a confident cry
He will come to the pair
Of lost maidens and fetch them away

Still safe in our land.
   Or are they galloping
Out to the westering
Brown of White Oea and over the pasture-lands,
Chariot-wheels thundering?
Into our hands
Ares delivers it!
Great is our God of War!
Harness and shining bit
Flashing, the sons of Colonus will ride
Full-tilt at the side
Of the knighthood of Athens,
The pride of the people who follow
Theseus the king,

   In honour of thee,
Athena, whose name
Is great among horsemen,
And thee whom they claim,
Earthshaker, the Lord of the Sea,
Whom the Earth-mother bore.

(A pause)

Are they fighting now,
Or do they stay?
Hope beguiles me, we shall see
Soon restored the unhappy victims
Of their kinsman's cruelty.
God is with us: something tells me
We have won the day.
O for the wings of a swift-soaring dove,
Wind-borne to ride above
The clouds and see the fray!

   Zeus, who seest all,
Great God on high!
Prosper in their enterprise
Our land's defenders with the strength

Thy all-conquering hand supplies.
And may thy daughter, the august
Athena, now be nigh.
Phoebus, and she who hunts the dappled deer,
His sister Queen, now hear
And help; our people cry.

CHORUS (*one of them, who has been standing apart, watching for further developments*): Now, wanderer, trust me for a true prophet; seeing is believing and here come the women, in safe hands.

OEDIPUS: Where, where? Is it true?

Enter ANTIGONE, ISMENE, THESEUS, *and attendants.*

ANTIGONE: Father! O that some god could make you see
This brave good man who has brought us back to you.

OEDIPUS: Child, is it you?

ANTIGONE: Yes, it was these strong hands
Of Theseus that saved us, with his trusty friends.

OEDIPUS: Come to me, child. Let me embrace the body
I never thought to touch again.

ANTIGONE: You shall.
It is what I long for too.

OEDIPUS: Where are you, then?

ANTIGONE: We are both together with you now.

OEDIPUS: My darlings!

ANTIGONE: The love in a father's heart!

OEDIPUS: So lost without you ...

ANTIGONE: All we have shared together ...

OEDIPUS: Mine again ...
Now I could die happy with you beside me.
Stay close, one to each arm, and cling again
To your loving father. I was lost and lonely.
But that must be no more ...
Tell me now, shortly,
What happened to you. Young lips need not be eloquent.

ANTIGONE: Let our deliverer tell you; it was his work;
The story shall be his, not mine.

OEDIPUS (*turning to* THESEUS): My friend,
   Forgive this long fond greeting to these children,
   Restored to me when I had thought them lost.
   I know it is only to you I owe this happiness.
   They owe their life to you. May God reward you,
   And your dear country; nowhere else but here
   Have I found justice, godliness, and truth.
   I know how much I have to thank you for.
   All that I have is of your giving, yours.
   Give me your hand, my lord. And may I kiss
   Your cheek?
      (*he is about to touch* THESEUS, *but suddenly withdraws*).
   No, no: I am a man of misery,
   Corrupt with every foulness that exists!
   I cannot let you touch me. No, you shall not!
   No one but those on whom it lies already
   Can bear this heavy load with me. Stay then
                  (*keeping* THESEUS *at a distance*)
   And take my thanks, so. And be kind to me
   Henceforth, as you are now.
THESEUS: There is nothing strange
   In your long and joyful welcome to your children.
   That your first thought should be for them, not me,
   Needs no apology. Not words, but deeds
   Are the goal of my ambition; as you may see;
   I have performed my promise, have I not?
   And here I am with your daughters safe and sound.
   How it was done – no need to speak of that –
   You'll hear it all from them.
   But listen, sir:
   On my way back, another piece of news
   Came to my ears, on which you can advise me:
   Not a long story, but it's curious,
   And man must be ever on his guard.
OEDIPUS: What is that, sir?
   We have heard nothing.

THESEUS: At Poseidon's altar,
  The very place where I was worshipping
  When the summons called me here, a man now sits,
  A suppliant. How he came there no one knows,
  But it seems he is of your kin, though not from Thebes.
OEDIPUS: Where does he come from? And what is his sup-
        plication?
THESEUS: I only know what they have told me of him;
  He asks a word with you, no more than that.
OEDIPUS: A suppliant – and only for a word?
THESEUS: That was the message – a word or two with you,
  And his safe passport home the way he came.
OEDIPUS: A suppliant at the altar? Who can he be?
THESEUS: Have you a kinsman, who might thus approach
  From Argos, say, or –   [you?
OEDIPUS (in horror): O my beloved friend!
  Say nothing more!
THESEUS: What is it?
OEDIPUS: Do not ask!
THESEUS: Not ask? Why, tell me –
OEDIPUS: Now I know the man.
THESEUS: Who, then? And have I any quarrel with him?
OEDIPUS: It is my son, sir! My worst enemy!
  The man whose voice I would most hate to hear.
THESEUS:
  Could you not hear him, though you do nothing for him
  Against your will? Could you not bear to hear him?
OEDIPUS: I am his father, but I tell you, sir,
  His very voice would be intolerable.
  Do not compel me to this necessity.
THESEUS: Are you not bound by his state of supplication?
  Respect for the god must be considered.
ANTIGONE: Father,
  Please listen to me, although I am young to advise you.
  Let the King do as he desires, for his own and the god's sake;
  Ismene and I would like our brother to come.

You needn't be afraid that anything he can say
That is not for your good will shake you from your
It cannot hurt you to hear him : just the reverse :　　[purpose.
Evil intentions betray themselves in speech.
You *are* his father ; and it cannot be right,
Even if he has done you the cruellest, wickedest wrong,
For you to do him wrong again.
Let him come.
Many a father has wayward sons to vex him,
But soothing friends can charm them out of anger.
Forget the present, and remember the old hard things
That happened to you on account of your father and
　　　　mother.
Will *they* not remind you what evil consequences
Come out of angry impulse? I think they must,
With the lesson in your sightless eyes.
To please us, father,
Say yes. You cannot refuse this fair request.
You have been well treated ; you cannot refuse to be
In making this return.　　　　　　　　　　[generous

OEDIPUS: My child, it is hard.
But I agree. So let it be as you wish.
(*To* THESEUS)
But O my friend, if the man is to come to us,
I charge you, guard my life!

THESEUS: As I have told you, sir, you need not fear.
I make no boasts, but while my life is safe,
You need not fear for yours.

Exit.

CHORUS:
Show me the man who asks an over-abundant share
Of life, in love with more, and ill content
With less, and I will show you one in love
With foolishness.
In the accumulation of many years
Pain is in plenty, and joy not anywhere

When life is over-spent.
And at the last there is the same release
When Death appears,
Unheralded by music, dance, or song,
To give us peace.

Say what you will, the greatest boon is not to be;
But, life begun, soonest to end is best,
And to that bourne from which our way began
Swiftly return.
The simple playtime of our youth behind,
What woe is absent, what fierce agony?
Strife, and the bloody test
Of battle, envy and hatred – and at length
Unloved, unkind,
Unfriended age, worst ill of all, and last,
Consumes our strength.

So stand, not I alone,
But all, and he,
Our much-tried friend,
A rock in a wild north sea
At winter's height,
Fronting the rude assault
Of all the billows of adversity
That break upon his head from every side
Unceasing – from the setting sun,
From dayspring, from the blaze of noon,
And from the pole of night.

ANTIGONE: There is someone coming now; I think it is he –
our visitor, father. He is alone, and weeping as he comes.

OEDIPUS: Who is it?

ANTIGONE: Just as we thought – Polynices. He is here.

Enter POLYNICES.

POLYNICES: O my sisters, my sisters! What can I say?
Which is the more to be pitied, I or my father,
For the unhappy plight I see him in: an exile

In this strange land, with only you beside him;
His dress – the old foul garments he has worn
To threadbare squalor on his ageing body;
Blind – and his white hair tousled by the breeze;
And just as beggarly the scanty victuals
He scrapes to satisfy his piteous hunger.
I know it now – too late! Wretch that I am!
I know, I admit I have treated you heartlessly;
I accuse myself, and need no other witness.
But Mercy sits beside the throne of God
And shares in all his dealings; so, my father,
May you yet come to know her. For what is done
There will be remedy; no worse can come.
No answer for me?
Speak, father; do not turn away. No answer?
No pity? You send me away without a word?
Not even to tell me why you are angry with me?
O sisters, cannot *you* persuade him to break
This hard unfeeling silence? I am a suppliant
For the god's good favour; he cannot neglect my petition
And let me go away unsatisfied.

> *He pauses, but* OEDIPUS *makes no response.*

ANTIGONE:
Say more, if you can, of the favour you came to ask.
As you talk, some tenderness may touch his heart;
Or even a word of anger or pity may draw
An answer out of silence.

POLYNICES: Well, I will.
But I claim the protection of the god; it was at his altar
The King of this country found me and gave me leave
To speak and be answered and go my way unharmed.
I ask you, friends, to uphold my right in this,
And you, my sisters, and my father ...

> (OEDIPUS *is still adamant, but* POLYNICES *continues*
> *with growing confidence*).

My father ...

Listen to the reason why I am here.
I am an exile, driven from the fatherland.
Because I claimed my birthright, the right to sit
In the seat of your former sovereignty, my brother,
My younger brother, Eteocles, expelled me.
The case was never argued; there was no fight;
But somehow he got the city on his side.
I suppose it was due to the curse upon your name;
And the oracles I have consulted bear this out.
It was then I went to Argos in Dorian country,
And married Adrastus' daughter, and made sworn allies
Of all the best-known fighters of Peloponnese,
With whom I planned my sevenfold league of offence
On Thebes, determined to drive the usurper out
Or die with honour.
      Now then, why am I here?
I am here to bring you, father, our earnest petition –
Mine and my friends' – seven of them, each with his army,
At this very moment encircling the Theban plain;
To wit: Amphiaráus, a mighty hand
With a spear, and our foremost master of augury;
Tydeus of Aetolia, Oineus' son; Eteoclus,
Of Argive birth; Hippomedon, representing
His father Talaos; Capaneus – he's for reducing
Thebes to a pile of cinders; Parthenopaeus,
A keen Arcadian, named after Atalanta
(Long time a virgin until she became the mother
Of this right trusty lad); and lastly, I
Who lead this doughty band to Thebes – your son
In name at least – or must I call myself
A son of hideous destiny?
      Now, father,
It is the earnest prayer of all this company,
For the sake of your daughters, for your own life's sake,
That you resign this anger you cherish against me
Now, as I go forth on my quest for vengeance

Against the brother who has supplanted me.
If oracles are true, the victory
 Will lie with those that win your patronage.
Hear me, my father; if you love our land
Of springing waters, if you love the gods
That gave us birth, hear my petition, father.
Both you and I are homeless outcasts, both
Condemned alike to beg for hospitality,
While the usurper, lording it at home,
Laughs at us both. My blood revolts at it!
But, with your blessing on my enterprise,
I'll send him packing; and when we're rid of him,
I shall restore you to your rightful place,
And take my own. With your consent I win
Certain success; without it, certain death.

CHORUS: Oedipus, for Theseus' sake, he must not go
 Till you have spoken what is in your mind.

OEDIPUS:
Gentlemen; were it not Theseus that sent him here,
Desiring me to speak to him, he should die
Before he heard a single word from me.
But he shall have his due; and what he hears
Shall be small comfort to him.
(*To* POLYNICES) Listen, scoundrel!
You held the sceptre and the royal throne
Before your brother seized them, and it was you
That drove your father out of doors. *You* made him
A homeless vagabond; this is *your* gift,
This pauperhood, at which you affect to weep,
Finding yourself in the same predicament.
It is no time for tears. This is my life
To bear till life is ended, and my death
Is on your head. You yoked me to this burden,
You banished me, you taught me how to beg;
You would have seen me dead, but I had daughters
Whose never-failing care has nursed my life.

They are my sons; you are some other man's.
   The eye of Fate is on you, and her wrath
Will visit you yet more nearly, if it is true
Your armies are in train for Thebes. That city
Will never fall to you; but you shall fall,
You and your brother, with blood on both your heads.
I cursed you once before; I curse you now –
These are my weapons – that you may learn the lesson
Of piety to parents, and repent
Your insults to my blindness; you – such sons!
How different from these daughters! ... 'Supplication'?
'Claim to the throne'? My curse be on them too,
If old eternal Justice reigns with God.
   Away! You have no father here, vile brute!
And take this malediction in your ears;
May you never defeat your motherland;
May you never return alive to Argos;
May you, in dying, kill your banisher,
And, killing, die by him who shares your blood.
This is my prayer.
In the name of the Father of Darkness, and the bottomless
   pit
Where he shall house you; in the name of the Goddesses
Whose ground we stand on; in the name of the Lord of
   Destruction
Who flung you into mortal strife. Now go:
And tell it out in all the streets of Thebes,
And tell your trusty friends, what benefactions
King Oedipus has bestowed upon his sons.

CHORUS: Go, Polynices. Your ways have all been evil.
   Go, without more ado.

POLYNICES: All this for nothing!
And worse than nothing. All those trusting friends,
And the high hopes in which we marched from Argos,
Brought to this end! An end I dare not name
To any of them. I cannot turn them back.

I must go on in silence to what awaits me.
But O my sisters, if all these pitiless curses
Which you have heard, fulfil themselves in act,
And if you ever come again to Thebes,
By all the gods, remember me with kindness.
Give me a grave, and reverent offices.
So to the commendation which you earn
For faithful service here, more may be added
By what you do for me.

ANTIGONE: O Polynices,
Do this one thing for me.

POLYNICES: What, dear Antigone?

ANTIGONE: Order your army back to Argos; now,
Before it is too late, to save yourself
And our city from destruction.

POLYNICES: That is impossible.
If I cry off this time, how can I ever
Lead them to battle again?

ANTIGONE: Again? But why?
Why need you fight again? What use is it
To make your home a ruin?

POLYNICES: Am I to endure
The insult of exile, and the mockery of a younger brother?

ANTIGONE: You are only hastening to its consummation
That double death your father prophesies.

POLYNICES: The deaths he hopes for! No, I'll not go back.

ANTIGONE: The more's the pity. How many of your men
Will follow when they hear what is foretold?

POLYNICES: They will not hear; I wouldn't tell such tales.
The careful leader does not spread alarm
By publishing bad news unnecessarily.

ANTIGONE: Then you're determined to do this?

POLYNICES: I am.
So let me go. I see my way before me,
Dark though it is and shadowed with grim shapes
Of vengeance answering to my father's prayers.

May yours be brighter, by God's mercy, sisters,
As you discharge that service at my death,
The last I shall require.
Now let me go.
This is good-bye for ever.

ANTIGONE: O my brother!
POLYNICES: Don't weep for me.
ANTIGONE: What can I do but weep,
Seeing you go like this to certain death?
POLYNICES: If certain, I must meet it.
ANTIGONE: Is there no other –?
POLYNICES: No other way that's right.
ANTIGONE: I cannot bear it!
To lose you!
POLYNICES: That must be as Fate decides.
Well ... May the gods be good to you. God knows
You have deserved it.

Exit.

CHORUS: More and more misfortune follows
From the blind man's indignation.
Or the hand of Fate directs it.
Who can say God's purpose falters?
Time is awake, the Wheel is turning,
Lifting up and overthrowing.

A distant peal of thunder.

Thunder in the roof of heaven!

OEDIPUS (*in great anxiety*): Dear children, the brave Theseus
should be here. Is there a messenger who could go to
fetch him?

ANTIGONE: For what purpose, father?

OEDIPUS: God is sending his voice across the sky to summon
me to death. Fetch Theseus quickly, quickly.

Thunder nearer.

CHORUS: Hear the heavens clamour, louder
Peals the volley of God's thunder.

Lightning.

And again the sky-fire, sending
Terror to the scalp flesh-creeping.
To what ending? Never idle
Is such loud assault or aimless.

Thunder very loud.

O great heaven! O God, have mercy!

OEDIPUS: Children, your father's life is drawing to its appointed end. There is no turning back.

ANTIGONE:

How do you know it, father? Have you a sign?

OEDIPUS: I know it well. The king, the king – let someone fetch him quickly.

Thunder.

CHORUS: Again the shattering din above us!
Merciful God, have mercy on us.
Spare us, if thou visitest
Our motherland with angry darkness.
Spare us; make not unavailing
All our pains for one forsaken.

Thunder.

Zeus, Lord, hear us cry!

OEDIPUS: Is he coming? How long? Will he come before I die? Before my mind is darkened?

ANTIGONE: What reassurance does it look for?

OEDIPUS: I promised him a blessing for what he has done for me. I want to make that promise good.

CHORUS: Royal prince! O quickly come, lad,
Even from Poseidon's altar ...
Is he worshipping the Sea-god
In the distant sanctuary? ...
Come, to take the stranger's blessing
On us all and on our city.

Thunder.

Quickly, royal master, come!

Enter THESEUS.

THESEUS: What urgent summons this time from you all? ...

I understand. Our guest has need of me.
Is it the threatening storm, the sky ablaze
With God's artillery? We may well be anxious
With heaven in this uproar.

OEDIPUS: O my king!
You are come as I desired, and that you are come
Is blessing sent from heaven on your head.

THESEUS: What is it, son of Laius?

OEDIPUS: My hour is near.
I must not die unfaithful to my pact
With you and with your city.

THESEUS: What is the sign
By which you know this crisis to be close?

OEDIPUS: The gods, themselves their own true couriers,
Have given me word by signals pre-appointed.

THESEUS: What signals do you mean, sir?

OEDIPUS: Peals of thunder,
Discharging meteors, many times repeated,
The armoury of the invincible.

THESEUS: I believe it.
Having cause to know the truth of your predictions.
What must I do?

Solemnly OEDIPUS *takes* THESEUS *aside.*

OEDIPUS: Son of Aegeus, what I have now to unfold
Is a thing that your city shall keep in its secret heart
Alive to the end of time. Soon I shall take you,
None guiding me, to the place where I must die;
And no one else must know it. Tell no man
The region where it lies concealed from sight,
That it may be for you henceforth for ever
A source of strength greater than many thousands
Of yeomen shields or allied spears. What follows,
A holy mystery that no tongue may name,
You shall then see and know, coming alone
To the place appointed. There is no one else
Of all this people to whom I can reveal it;

Not my own children, though I love them well.
You are to keep it for ever, you alone;
And when your life is drawing to its end,
Disclose it to one alone, your chosen heir,
And he to his, and so for ever and ever.
This will insure your city's safe defence
Against the power of the Sons of the Dragon's Seed.
Between city and city, be they never so justly ruled,
Occasions are never wanting for thoughtless insult.
The gods take notice, in their own good time,
But without fail, when godliness is flouted
And men go mad. Let it not happen to you,
O son of Aegeus. But there, I do not think
You need my teaching.
Now it is time to go.
The hand of God directs me.

> *He turns, and leads the way with slow but sure steps,*
> *as one inspired with inward vision.*

Follow, my children.
It is my turn now to be your pathfinder,
As you have been to me. Come. Do not touch me.
Leave me to find the way to the sacred grave
Where this land's soil is to enclose my bones.
This way ... This way ... Hermes is leading me,
And the Queen of the Nether World. This way ... This way.

> *He turns to feel the sunlight for the last time upon his*
> *face and hands.*

Dark day! How long since thou wast light to me!
Farewell! I feel my last of thee. Death's night
Now ends my life for ever.
(*Turning once more to* THESEUS) Blessing attend
Your land and all that serve you, and yourself,
My best-loved friend; and in your blessedness,
That it may be yours for ever, remember me.

> *He goes, the others following; in prolonged silence the* CHORUS
> *watch the procession out of sight; then they pray.*

CHORUS:

> Goddess unseen, and Lord of the Sons of Darkness,
> Aidoneus! Aidoneus!
> If such petition may be heard:
> Grant to our friend a passing with no pain,
> No grief, to the dark Stygian home
> Of those who dwell in the far invisible land.
> Out of the night of his long hopeless torment
> Surely a just God's hand
> Will raise him up again.

> Have mercy, Infernal Powers; famed Hound of Hell,
> Immovable invincible
> Grim sentinel in caverns howling
> Round the wide gates of hospitable Death:
> O Son of Earth and Hades, hear us.
> Let not the beast lie in the traveller's way,
> Who fares to the deep country of the dead.
> Bear him with gentle breath,
> O endless sleep, away.

After a long pause, a MESSENGER *returns from the direction taken by* OEDIPUS.

MESSENGER: People of Colonus! I am here to say that the life of Oedipus is ended. And there is much to tell of all that I saw happen there.

CHORUS: He is dead, poor soul?

MESSENGER: He has seen the last of his mortal days.

CHORUS: By some act of God, was it? And with no pain?

MESSENGER: It was wonderful.

> You all know how he left this place; you saw how he refused the guidance of his friends, but led us all boldly forward. He went on as far as the brink of the Chasm, where the Brazen Staircase plunges into the roots of the earth – near the rock-basin which commemorates the famous covenant of Theseus and Peirithous. There he stood, among those hallowed objects – the Basin, the Rock of Thoricus, the Hol-

low Pear-tree, the Stone Tomb. He sat down; took off his toil-stained garments; and calling for his daughters, asked them to fetch water from the stream, so that he might wash and pour water-offerings. They went, towards the Hill of the Harvest-goddess, which lay in front of us; and soon returned bringing him what he asked for. Then they washed and dressed him after the customary manner.

When he was satisfied with all that had been done – and nothing was denied him – there came a peal of thunder, the voice of the God of Earth; and the women trembled and wept, falling at their father's knees; and for a long time they lamented loudly and beat their breasts. Pained at their outcry, he took them in his arms and said: 'My children, to-day your father leaves you. This is the end of all that was I, and the end of your long task of caring for me. I know how hard it was. Yet it was made lighter by one word – love. I loved you as no one else had ever done. Now you must live on without me.'

So they wept, clinging to each other. And when they ended, there was silence; until suddenly a Voice called him, a terrifying voice at which all trembled and hair stood on end. A god was calling to him. 'Oedipus! Oedipus!' it cried, again and again. 'It is time: you stay too long.' He heard the summons, and knew that it was from God. Then he called for King Theseus, and when he was near him said: 'Dear friend, give your hand and promise to these children. Children, your hand in his. Promise never of your own will to forsake them, but do such things as you think fitting for their good, with all goodwill.' And Theseus, like the noble man he is, made no lament but took his oath to do as his friend desired.

When this was done, Oedipus again groped blindly for his children, and said: 'Now, my children, you must be brave and good, and go from this place. You must not ask to see forbidden mysteries; there are things you must not hear. Go quickly. Only Theseus is permitted to remain and see the rest.' We all heard this, and so, weeping bitterly, we and the women came away.

When we had gone a little distance, we turned and looked back. Oedipus was nowhere to be seen; but the King was standing alone holding his hand before his eyes as if he had seen some terrible sight that no one could bear to look upon; and soon we saw him salute heaven and the earth with one short prayer.

In what manner Oedipus passed from this earth, no one can tell. Only Theseus knows. We know he was not destroyed by a thunderbolt from heaven nor tide-wave rising from the sea, for no such thing occurred. Maybe a guiding spirit from the gods took him, or the earth's foundations gently opened and received him with no pain. Certain it is that he was taken without a pang, without grief or agony – a passing more wonderful than that of any other man.

What I have said will seem, perhaps, like some wild dream of fancy, beyond belief. If so, then you must disbelieve it. I can say no more.

CHORUS: Where are the women, and their escort?

MESSENGER: Not far behind. They are coming now, for I can hear their weeping.

Enter ANTIGONE *and* ISMENE.

ANTIGONE: Now all is done. For us nothing remains
But to weep for ever and ever the curse of our blood.
While he was here, we helped him to bear it;
But now, what we have seen and suffered
At the end, is beyond all understanding.

CHORUS: What happened?

ANTIGONE: We only guess.

CHORUS: He died?

ANTIGONE: As you would have wished for him;
Not in the peril of war,
Nor in the sea;
But by a swift invisible hand
He was lifted away to the far dark shore.

And dark as death shall our night be.
How shall we live? What far-off land
Or ocean must be the bourne
Of our long misery?

ISMENE: I cannot tell; and O that I could lie
In death beside him, and not live
The life that will be mine.

CHORUS: Most faithful daughters, is it not best to bear
What God's hand brings?
This grief must not burn in you overlong;
Your part has been beyond all blame.

ANTIGONE: I never knew how great the loss could be
Even of sadness; there was a sort of joy
In sorrow, when he was at my side.
Father, my love, in your shroud of earth
We two shall love you for ever and ever.

CHORUS: He is happy?

ANTIGONE: He has his wish.

CHORUS: His wish?

ANTIGONE: He came to a land he loved
In its cool curtained bed
Of earth to lie.
And here are tears for him; but how
Shall all the tears these eyes have shed
Put this so heavy sorrow by?
As he had wished, in strange earth now
He sleeps, and I must not know
Where they have laid his head.

ISMENE: And what will become of us, now he is gone?
Sad sisters, what will our fate be
Without a father near?

CHORUS: Be sure his end was happy, and your grief
Must not be endless.
No man has ever lived out of the reach
Of misadventure's grasping hand.

ANTIGONE: Sister, we must go back.

ISMENE: Go back?
ANTIGONE: I must, I must.
ISMENE: But why?
ANTIGONE: To see the plot of earth –
ISMENE: His?
ANTIGONE: Father's – I cannot leave him –
ISMENE: It is forbidden. Surely you understand?
ANTIGONE: Why do you cross me?
ISMENE: Don't you see?
ANTIGONE: See?
ISMENE: He had to die alone, and has no tomb.
ANTIGONE: Take me to the place and let me die there too.
ISMENE: And what shall I do all alone and helpless?
Where shall I live without a friend?
CHORUS: You must not fear.
ISMENE: And where shall I be safe?
CHORUS: You are safe already.
ISMENE: How?
CHORUS: You are in safe hands.
ISMENE: I know.
CHORUS: Then what is in your mind?
ISMENE: How shall we ever see home again?
CHORUS: Do not attempt it.
ISMENE: Trouble on every side.
CHORUS: The worst is past.
ISMENE: And more is added to that worst.
CHORUS: Deep waters of adversity, in truth.
ISMENE: O where, O where, O God?
Where is there any hope?

Enter THESEUS

THESEUS: Now, daughters, dry your tears. Kind death
Has gently dealt with him; and we
Share in his blessing. We must not weep;
Our grief would provoke the gods to anger.
ANTIGONE: Yet hear a petition, son of Aegeus.
THESEUS: What is it you ask?

ANTIGONE: Only to see
  Our father's grave.
THESEUS: That cannot be.
ANTIGONE: Why? You are lord of Athens. Why?
THESEUS: Daughters, it was your father's charge
  That no man should approach that place,
  Nor any living voice be heard
  About the sacred sepulchre
  In which he sleeps; this pact obeyed
  Preserves this land inviolate.
  I swore it, and God's sentinel
  Saw, who sees all, and took my oath.
ANTIGONE: It was his wish. It is enough.
  Then pray you see us safe returned
  To age-old Thebes. There it may be
  We can yet stem the tide of blood
  That dooms our brothers.
THESEUS: It shall be done.
  I cannot rest till I have served
  Your good in everything, and his,
  The lately lost, who lies below.
CHORUS: This is the end of tears:
  No more lament.
  Through all the years
  Immutable stands this event.

EXEUNT

THE LEGEND CONTINUED

*So Oedipus passed from mortal sight, and while his soul was received
into the blessed abodes, his earthly remains, in the secret keeping of
King Theseus, hallowed for all time the Attic soil in which they
rested.*

    *Meanwhile the strife between his sons went on with unabated fury.
Seven champions, enlisted under the banner of Polynices, stormed
with his Argive allies the seven gates of Thebes. But Thebes with-
stood them, and in the last encounter the two brothers took each other's
life. Creon, now once more undisputed master of the city, and resolved to make an example of the iniquity of the invader, ordered that
whilst the body of Eteocles, defender of the city, received all honourable rites of burial, that of Polynices should be left in ignominy, unwept and unburied, upon the plain where it lay. Penalty of death was
promulgated against any who should defy this order; and the voices
of the city, whether in consent or in fearful submission, were silent.*

[Here the play of ANTIGONE begins]

ANTIGONE

*

CHARACTERS

Ismene ⎫ *daughters of Oedipus*
Antigone ⎭
Creon, *King of Thebes*
Haemon, *son of Creon*
Teiresias, *a blind prophet*
A Sentry
A Messenger
Eurydice, *wife of Creon*
Chorus *of Theban elders*
King's attendants
Queen's attendants
A boy leading Teiresias
Soldiers

*

Scene: Before the Palace at Thebes

Enter ISMENE *from the central door of the Palace.* ANTIGONE
*follows, anxious and urgent; she closes the door carefully, and
comes to join her sister.*

ANTIGONE: O sister! Ismene dear, dear sister Ismene!
    You know how heavy the hand of God is upon us;
    How we who are left must suffer for our father, Oedipus.
    There is no pain, no sorrow, no suffering, no dishonour
    We have not shared together, you and I.
    And now there is something more. Have you heard this
        order,
    This latest order that the King has proclaimed to the city?
    Have you heard how our dearest are being treated like
        enemies?
ISMENE: I have heard nothing about any of those we love,

Neither good nor evil – not, I mean, since the death
Of our two brothers, both fallen in a day.
The Argive army, I hear, was withdrawn last night.
I know no more to make me sad or glad.

ANTIGONE:
I thought you did not. That's why I brought you out here,
Where we shan't be heard, to tell you something alone.

ISMENE:
What is it, Antigone? Black news, I can see already.

ANTIGONE:
O Ismene, what do you think? Our two dear brothers ...
Creon has given funeral honours to one,
And not to the other; nothing but shame and ignominy.
Eteocles has been buried, they tell me, in state,
With all honourable observances due to the dead.
But Polynices, just as unhappily fallen – the order
Says he is not to be buried, not to be mourned;
To be left unburied, unwept, a feast of flesh
For keen-eyed carrion birds. The noble Creon!
It is against you and me he has made this order.
Yes, against me. And soon he will be here himself
To make it plain to those that have not heard it,
And to enforce it. This is no idle threat;
The punishment for disobedience is death by stoning.
So now you know. And now is the time to show
Whether or not you are worthy of your high blood.

ISMENE: My poor Antigone, if this is really true,
What more can I do, or undo, to help you?

ANTIGONE:
Will you help me? Will you do something with me? Will
    you?

ISMENE: Help you do what, Antigone? What do you mean?

ANTIGONE:
Would you help me lift the body ... you and me?

ISMENE:
You cannot mean ... to bury him? Against the order?

ANTIGONE:
Is he not my brother, and yours, whether you like it
Or not? *I* shall never desert him, never.

ISMENE:
How could you dare, when Creon has expressly forbidden it?

ANTIGONE: He has no right to keep me from my own.

ISMENE: O sister, sister, do you forget how our father
Perished in shame and misery, his awful sin
Self-proved, blinded by his own self-mutilation?
And then his mother, his wife – for she was both –
Destroyed herself in a noose of her own making.
And now our brothers, both in a single day
Fallen in an awful exaction of death for death,
Blood for blood, each slain by the other's hand.
Now we two left; and what will be the end of us,
If we transgress the law and defy our king?
O think, Antigone; we are women; it is not for us
To fight against men; our rulers are stronger than we,
And we must obey in this, or in worse than this.
May the dead forgive me, I can do no other
But as I am commanded; to do more is madness.

ANTIGONE: No; then I will not ask you for your help.
Nor would I thank you for it, if you gave it.
Go your own way; I will bury my brother;
And if I die for it, what happiness!
Convicted of reverence – I shall be content
To lie beside a brother whom I love.
We have only a little time to please the living,
But all eternity to love the dead.
There I shall lie for ever. Live, if you will;
Live, and defy the holiest laws of heaven.

ISMENE: I do not defy them; but I cannot act
Against the State. I am not strong enough.

ANTIGONE: Let that be your excuse, then. I will go
And heap a mound of earth over my brother.

ISMENE: I fear for you, Antigone; I fear –

ANTIGONE: You need not fear for me. Fear for yourself.

ISMENE: At least be secret. Do not breathe a word.
  I'll not betray your secret.

ANTIGONE: Publish it
  To all the world! Else I shall hate you more.

ISMENE: Your heart burns! Mine is frozen at the thought.

ANTIGONE: I know my duty, where true duty lies.

ISMENE: If you can do it; but you're bound to fail.

ANTIGONE: When I have *tried* and failed, I shall have failed.

ISMENE: No sense in starting on a hopeless task.

ANTIGONE: Oh, I shall hate you if you talk like that!
  And *he* will hate you, rightly. Leave me alone
  With my own madness. There is no punishment
  Can rob me of my honourable death.

ISMENE: Go then, if you are determined, to your folly.
  But remember that those who love you ... love you still.

ISMENE *goes into the Palace.*

ANTIGONE *leaves the stage by a side exit.*

Enter the CHORUS *of Theban elders.*

CHORUS:
  Hail the sun! the brightest of all that ever
  Dawned on the City of Seven Gates, City of Thebes!
  Hail the golden dawn over Dirce's river
  Rising to speed the flight of the white invaders
      Homeward in full retreat!

  The army of Polynices was gathered against us,
  In angry dispute his voice was lifted against us,
  Like a ravening bird of prey he swooped around us
  With white wings flashing, with flying plumes,
      With armed hosts ranked in thousands.

  At the threshold of seven gates in a circle of blood
  His swords stood round us, his jaws were opened against us;
  But before he could taste our blood, or consume us with
  He fled, fled with the roar of the dragon behind him [fire,
      And thunder of war in his ears.

E

The Father of Heaven abhors the proud tongue's boasting;
He marked the oncoming torrent, the flashing stream
Of their golden harness, the clash of their battle gear;
He heard the invader cry Victory over our ramparts,
    And smote him with fire to the ground.

Down to the ground from the crest of his hurricane
    onslaught
He swung, with the fiery brands of his hate brought low:
Each and all to their doom of destruction appointed
    By the god that fighteth for us.

Seven invaders at seven gates seven defenders
Spoiled of their bronze for a tribute to Zeus; save two
Luckless brothers in one fight matched together
    And in one death laid low.

Great is the victory, great be the joy
In the city of Thebes, the city of chariots.
Now is the time to fill the temples
With glad thanksgiving for warfare ended;
Shake the ground with the night-long dances,
Bacchus afoot and delight abounding.

But see, the King comes here,
Creon, the son of Menoeceus,
Whom the gods have appointed for us
In our recent change of fortune.
What matter is it, I wonder,
That has led him to call us together
By his special proclamation?

The central door is opened, and CREON *enters.*

CREON:
My councillors: now that the gods have brought our city
Safe through a storm of trouble to tranquillity,
I have called you especially out of all my people
To conference together, knowing that you
Were loyal subjects when King Laius reigned,

And when King Oedipus so wisely ruled us,
And again, upon his death, faithfully served
His sons, till they in turn fell – both slayers, both slain,
Both stained with brother-blood, dead in a day –
And I, their next of kin, inherited
The throne and kingdom which I now possess.

    No other touchstone can test the heart of a man,
The temper of his mind and spirit, till he be tried
In the practice of authority and rule.
For my part, I have always held the view,
And hold it still, that a king whose lips are sealed
By fear, unwilling to seek advice, is damned.
And no less damned is he who puts a friend
Above his country; I have no good word for him.
As God above is my witness, who sees all,
When I see any danger threatening my people,
Whatever it may be, I shall declare it.
No man who is his country's enemy
Shall call himself my friend. Of this I am sure –
Our country is our life; only when she
Rides safely, have we any friends at all.
Such is my policy for our common weal.

    In pursuance of this, I have made a proclamation
Concerning the sons of Oedipus, as follows:
Eteocles, who fell fighting in defence of the city,
Fighting gallantly, is to be honoured with burial
And with all the rites due to the noble dead.
The other – you know whom I mean – his brother Polynices,
Who came back from exile intending to burn and destroy
His fatherland and the gods of his fatherland,
To drink the blood of his kin, to make them slaves –
He is to have no grave, no burial,
No mourning from anyone; it is forbidden.
He is to be left unburied, left to be eaten
By dogs and vultures, a horror for all to see.
I am determined that never, if I can help it,

    Shall evil triumph over good. Alive
    Or dead, the faithful servant of his country
    Shall be rewarded.

CHORUS: Creon, son of Menoeceus,
    You have given your judgment for the friend and for the
        enemy.
    As for those that are dead, so for us who remain,
    Your will is law.

CREON: See then that it be kept.

CHORUS: My lord, some younger would be fitter for that

CREON: Watchers are already set over the corpse.   [task.

CHORUS: What other duty then remains for us?

CREON: Not to connive at any disobedience.

CHORUS: If there were any so mad as to ask for death –

CREON: Ay, that is the penalty. There is always someone
    Ready to be lured to ruin by hope of gain.

    He turns to go. A SENTRY *enters from the side of the stage.*
            CREON *pauses at the Palace door.*

SENTRY:
    My lord: if I am out of breath, it is not from haste.
    I have not been running. On the contrary, many a time
    I stopped to think and loitered on the way,
    Saying to myself 'Why hurry to your doom,
    Poor fool?' and then I said 'Hurry, you fool.
    If Creon hears this from another man,
    Your head's as good as off.' So here I am,
    As quick as my unwilling haste could bring me;
    In no great hurry, in fact. So now I am here ...
    But I'll tell my story ... though it may be nothing after all.
    And whatever I have to suffer, it can't be more
    Than what God wills, so I cling to that for my comfort.

CREON: Good heavens, man, whatever is the matter?

SENTRY: To speak of myself first – I never did it, sir;
    Nor saw who did; no one can punish me for that.

CREON: You tell your story with a deal of artful precaution.
    It's evidently something strange.

SENTRY: It is.

So strange, it's very difficult to tell.

CREON: Well, out with it, and let's be done with you.

SENTRY: It's this, sir. The corpse ... someone has just

Buried it and gone. Dry dust over the body

They scattered, in the manner of holy burial.

CREON: What! Who dared to do it?

SENTRY: I don't know, sir.

There was no sign of a pick, no scratch of a shovel;

The ground was hard and dry – no trace of a wheel;

Whoever it was has left no clues behind him.

When the sentry on the first watch showed it us,

We were amazed. The corpse was covered from sight –

Not with a proper grave – just a layer of earth –

As it might be, the act of some pious passer-by.

There were no tracks of an animal either, a dog

Or anything that might have come and mauled the body.

Of course we all started pitching in to each other,

Accusing each other, and might have come to blows,

With no one to stop us; for anyone might have done it,

But it couldn't be proved against him, and all denied it.

We were all ready to take hot iron in hand

And go through fire and swear by God and heaven

We hadn't done it, nor knew of anyone

That could have thought of doing it, much less done it.

Well, we could make nothing of it. Then one of our men

Said something that made all our blood run cold –

Something we could neither refuse to do, nor do,

But at our own risk. What he said was 'This

Must be reported to the King; we can't conceal it.'

So it was agreed. We drew lots for it, and I,

Such is my luck, was chosen. So here I am,

As much against my will as yours, I'm sure;

A bringer of bad news expects no welcome.

CHORUS: My lord, I fear – I feared it from the first –

That this may prove to be an act of the gods.

CREON: Enough of that! Or I shall lose my patience.
   Don't talk like an old fool, old though you be.
   Blasphemy, to say the gods could give a thought
   To carrion flesh! Held him in high esteem,
   I suppose, and buried him like a benefactor –
   A man who came to burn their temples down,
   Ransack their holy shrines, their land, their laws?
   Is that the sort of man you think gods love?
   Not they. No. There's a party of malcontents
   In the city, rebels against my word and law,
   Shakers of heads in secret, impatient of rule;
   They are the people, I see it well enough,
   Who have bribed their instruments to do this thing.
   Money! Money's the curse of man, none greater.
   That's what wrecks cities, banishes men from home,
   Tempts and deludes the most well-meaning soul,
   Pointing out the way to infamy and shame.
   Well, they shall pay for their success.
   (*To the* SENTRY)
   See to it!
   See to it, you! Upon my oath, I swear,
   As Zeus is my god above: either you find
   The perpetrator of this burial
   And bring him here into my sight, or death –
   No, not your mere death shall pay the reckoning,
   But, for a living lesson against such infamy,
   You shall be racked and tortured till you tell
   The whole truth of this outrage; so you may learn
   To seek your gain where gain is yours to get,
   Not try to grasp it everywhere. In wickedness
   You'll find more loss than profit.
SENTRY: May I say more?
CREON: No more; each word you say but stings me more.
SENTRY: Stings in your ears, sir, or in your deeper feelings?
CREON: Don't bandy words, fellow, about my feelings.
SENTRY: Though I offend your ears, sir, it is not I

But he that's guilty that offends your soul.
CREON: Oh, born to argue, were you?
SENTRY: Maybe so;
  But still not guilty in this business.
CREON: Doubly so, if you have sold your soul for money.
SENTRY:
  To think that thinking men should think so wrongly!
CREON: Think what you will. But if you fail to find
  The doer of this deed, you'll learn one thing:
  Ill-gotten gain brings no one any good.

                    He goes into the Palace.

SENTRY: Well, heaven send they find him. But whether or
  They'll not find me again, that's sure. Once free,   [no,
  Who never thought to see another day,
  I'll thank my lucky stars, and keep away.

                    Exit.

CHORUS:
  Wonders are many on earth, and the greatest of these
  Is man, who rides the ocean and takes his way
  Through the deeps, through wind-swept valleys of perilous
      That surge and sway.   [seas

  He is master of ageless Earth, to his own will bending
  The immortal mother of gods by the sweat of his brow,
  As year succeeds to year, with toil unending
      Of mule and plough.

  He is lord of all things living; birds of the air,
  Beasts of the field, all creatures of sea and land
  He taketh, cunning to capture and ensnare
      With sleight of hand;

  Hunting the savage beast from the upland rocks,
  Taming the mountain monarch in his lair,
  Teaching the wild horse and the roaming ox
      His yoke to bear.

  The use of language, the wind-swift motion of brain
  He learnt; found out the laws of living together

In cities, building him shelter against the rain
    And wintry weather.

  There is nothing beyond his power. His subtlety
Meeteth all chance, all danger conquereth.
For every ill he hath found its remedy,
    Save only death.

  O wondrous subtlety of man, that draws
To good or evil ways! Great honour is given
And power to him who upholdeth his country's laws
    And the justice of heaven.

  But he that, too rashly daring, walks in sin
In solitary pride to his life's end.
At door of mine shall never enter in
    To call me friend.

  (*Severally, seeing some persons approach from a distance*)
O gods! A wonder to see!
Surely it cannot be –
It is no other –
Antigone!
Unhappy maid –
Unhappy Oedipus' daughter; it is she they bring.
Can she have rashly disobeyed
The order of our King?
      Enter the SENTRY, *bringing* ANTIGONE *guarded
      by two more soldiers.*

SENTRY: We've got her. Here's the woman that did the deed.
  We found her in the act of burying him. Where's the King?
CHORUS: He is just coming out of the palace now.
               Enter CREON.
CREON: What's this? What am I just in time to see?
SENTRY: My lord, an oath's a very dangerous thing.
  Second thoughts may prove us liars. Not long since
  I swore I wouldn't trust myself again
  To face your threats; you gave me a drubbing the first
  But there's no pleasure like an unexpected pleasure, [time.

Not by a long way. And so I've come again,
Though against my solemn oath. And I've brought this
    lady,
Who's been caught in the act of setting that grave in order.
And no casting lots for it this time – the prize is mine
And no one else's. So take her; judge and convict her.
I'm free, I hope, and quit of the horrible business.

CREON:
How did you find her? Where have you brought her from?

SENTRY:
She was burying the man with her own hands, and that's
    the truth.

CREON: Are you in your senses? Do you know what you are
    saying?

SENTRY: I saw her myself, burying the body of the man
Whom you said not to bury. Don't I speak plain?

CREON: How did she come to be seen and taken in the act?

SENTRY: It was this way.
After I got back to the place,
With all your threats and curses ringing in my ears,
We swept off all the earth that covered the body,
And left it a sodden naked corpse again;
Then sat up on the hill, on the windward side,
Keeping clear of the stench of him, as far as we could;
All of us keeping each other up to the mark,
With pretty sharp speaking, not to be caught napping this
So this went on some hours, till the flaming sun   [time.
Was high in the top of the sky, and the heat was blazing.
Suddenly a storm of dust, like a plague from heaven,
Swept over the ground, stripping the trees stark bare,
Filling the sky; you had to shut your eyes
To stand against it. When at last it stopped,
There was the girl, screaming like an angry bird,
When it finds its nest left empty and little ones gone.
Just like that she screamed, seeing the body
Naked, crying and cursing the ones that had done it.

Then she picks up the dry earth in her hands,
And pouring out of a fine bronze urn she's brought
She makes her offering three times to the dead.
Soon as we saw it, down we came and caught her.
She wasn't at all frightened. And so we charged her
With what she'd done before, and this. She admitted it,
I'm glad to say – though sorry too, in a way.
It's good to save your own skin, but a pity
To have to see another get into trouble,
Whom you've no grudge against. However, I can't say
I've ever valued anyone else's life
More than my own, and that's the honest truth.

CREON (to ANTIGONE): Well, what do you say – you, hiding
Do you admit, or do you deny the deed? [your head there:

ANTIGONE: I do admit it. I do not deny it.

CREON (to the SENTRY):
You – you may go. You are discharged from blame.
                    Exit SENTRY.
Now tell me, in as few words as you can,
Did you know the order forbidding such an act?

ANTIGONE: I knew it, naturally. It was plain enough.

CREON: And yet you dared to contravene it?

ANTIGONE: Yes.
That order did not come from God. Justice,
That dwells with the gods below, knows no such law.
I did not think your edicts strong enough
To overrule the unwritten unalterable laws
Of God and heaven, you being only a man.
They are not of yesterday or to-day, but everlasting,
Though where they came from, none of us can tell.
Guilty of their transgression before God
I cannot be, for any man on earth.
I knew that I should have to die, of course,
With or without your order. If it be soon,
So much the better. Living in daily torment
As I do, who would not be glad to die?

This punishment will not be any pain.
Only if I had let my mother's son
Lie there unburied, then I could not have borne it.
This I can bear. Does that seem foolish to you?
Or is it you that are foolish to judge me so?

CHORUS: She shows her father's stubborn spirit: foolish
Not to give way when everything's against her.

CREON: Ah, but you'll see. The over-obstinate spirit
Is soonest broken; as the strongest iron will snap
If over-tempered in the fire to brittleness.
A little halter is enough to break
The wildest horse. Proud thoughts do not sit well
Upon subordinates. This girl's proud spirit
Was first in evidence when she broke the law;
And now, to add insult to her injury,
She gloats over her deed. But, as I live,
She shall not flout my orders with impunity.
My sister's child – ay, were she even nearer,
Nearest and dearest, she should not escape
Full punishment – she, and her sister too,
Her partner, doubtless, in this burying.
    Let her be fetched! She was in the house just now;
I saw her, hardly in her right mind either.
Often the thoughts of those who plan dark deeds
Betray themselves before the deed is done.
The criminal who being caught still tries
To make a fair excuse, is damned indeed.

ANTIGONE:
Now you have caught, will you do more than kill me?

CREON: No, nothing more; that is all I could wish.

ANTIGONE:
Why then delay? There is nothing that you can say
That I should wish to hear, as nothing I say
Can weigh with you. I have given my brother burial.
What greater honour could I wish? All these
Would say that what I did was honourable,

But fear locks up their lips. To speak and act
Just as he likes is a king's prerogative.

CREON:

You are wrong. None of my subjects thinks as you do.

ANTIGONE: Yes, sir, they do; but dare not tell you so.

CREON: And you are not only alone, but unashamed.

ANTIGONE: There is no shame in honouring my brother.

CREON:

Was not his enemy, who died with him, your brother?

ANTIGONE:

Yes, both were brothers, both of the same parents.

CREON: You honour one, and so insult the other.

ANTIGONE: He that is dead will not accuse me of that.

CREON: He will, if you honour him no more than the traitor.

ANTIGONE:

It was not a slave, but his brother, that died with him.

CREON: Attacking his country, while the other defended it.

ANTIGONE: Even so, we have a duty to the dead.

CREON: Not to give equal honour to good and bad.

ANTIGONE: Who knows? In the country of the dead that
          may be the law.

CREON: An enemy can't be a friend, even when dead.

ANTIGONE: My way is to share my love, not share my hate.

CREON: Go then, and share your love among the dead.
       We'll have no woman's law here, while I live.

Enter ISMENE *from the Palace.*

CHORUS: Here comes Ismene, weeping
   In sisterly sorrow; a darkened brow,
   Flushed face, and the fair cheek marred
   With flooding rain.

CREON: You crawling viper! Lurking in my house
   To suck my blood! Two traitors unbeknown
   Plotting against my throne. Do you admit
   To a share in this burying, or deny all knowledge?

ISMENE: I did it – yes – if she will let me say so.
   I am as much to blame as she is.

ANTIGONE: No.
  That is not just. You would not lend a hand
  And I refused your help in what I did.

ISMENE: But I am not ashamed to stand beside you
  Now in your hour of trial, Antigone.

ANTIGONE:
  Whose was the deed, Death and the dead are witness.
  I love no friend whose love is only words.

ISMENE: O sister, sister, let me share your death,
  Share in the tribute of honour to him that is dead.

ANTIGONE: You shall not die with me. You shall not claim
  That which you would not touch. One death is enough.

ISMENE: How can I bear to live, if you must die?

ANTIGONE: Ask Creon. Is not he the one you care for?

ISMENE: You do yourself no good to taunt me so.

ANTIGONE: Indeed no: even my jests are bitter pains.

ISMENE: But how, O tell me, how can I still help you?

ANTIGONE: Help yourself. I shall not stand in your way.

ISMENE: For pity, Antigone – can I not die with you?

ANTIGONE:
  You chose; life was your choice, when mine was death.

ISMENE: Although I warned you that it would be so.

ANTIGONE: Your way seemed right to some, ﹍ others mine.

ISMENE: But now both in the wrong, and both condemned.

ANTIGONE: No, no. You live. My heart was long since
  So it was right for me to help the dead.   [dead,

CREON: I do believe the creatures both are mad;
  One lately crazed, the other from her birth.

ISMENE: Is it not likely, sir? The strongest mind
  Cannot but break under misfortune's blows.

CREON: Yours did, when you threw in your lot with hers.

ISMENE: How could I wish to live without my sister?

CREON: You have no sister. Count her dead already.

ISMENE: You could not take her – kill your own son's bride?

CREON: Oh, there are other fields for him to plough.

ISMENE: No truer troth was ever made than theirs.

CREON: No son of mine shall wed so vile a creature.

ANTIGONE: O Haemon, can your father spite you so?

CREON: You and your paramour, I hate you both.

CHORUS:
  Sir, would you take her from your own son's arms?

CREON: Not I, but death shall take her.

CHORUS: Be it so.
  Her death, it seems, is certain.

CREON: Certain it is.
  No more delay. Take them, and keep them within –
  The proper place for women. None so brave
  As not to look for some way of escape
  When they see life stand face to face with death.

                    The women are taken away.

CHORUS:
  Happy are they who know not the taste of evil.
  From a house that heaven hath shaken
  The curse departs not
  But falls upon all of the blood,
  Like the restless surge of the sea when the dark storm drives
  The black sand hurled from the deeps
  And the Thracian gales boom down
  On the echoing shore.

    In life and in death is the house of Labdacus stricken.
  Generation to generation,
  With no atonement,
  It is scourged by the wrath of a god.
  And now for the dead dust's sake is the light of promise,
  The tree's last root, crushed out
  By pride of heart and the sin
  Of presumptuous tongue.

    For what presumption of man can match thy power,
  O Zeus, that art not subject to sleep or time
  Or age, living for ever in bright Olympus?
  To-morrow and for all time to come,

As in the past,
This law is immutable:
For mortals greatly to live is greatly to suffer.

    Roving ambition helps many a man to good,
And many it falsely lures to light desires,
Till failure trips them unawares, and they fall
On the fire that consumes them. Well was it said,
Evil seems good
To him who is doomed to suffer;
And short is the time before that suffering comes.

    But here comes Haemon,
Your youngest son.
Does he come to speak his sorrow
For the doom of his promised bride,
The loss of his marriage hopes?

CREON:
  We shall know it soon, and need no prophet to tell us.
              Enter HAEMON.
  Son, you have heard, I think, our final judgment
  On your late betrothed. No angry words, I hope?
  Still friends, in spite of everything, my son?

HAEMON: I am your son, sir; by your wise decisions
  My life is ruled, and them I shall always obey.
  I cannot value any marriage-tie
  Above your own good guidance.

CREON: Rightly said.
  Your father's will should have your heart's first place.
  Only for this do fathers pray for sons
  Obedient, loyal, ready to strike down
  Their fathers' foes, and love their fathers' friends.
  To be the father of unprofitable sons
  Is to be the father of sorrows, a laughing-stock
  To all one's enemies. Do not be fooled, my son,
  By lust and the wiles of a woman. You'll have bought
  Cold comfort if your wife's a worthless one.

No wound strikes deeper than love that is turned to hate.
This girl's an enemy; away with her,
And let her go and find a mate in Hades.
Once having caught her in a flagrant act –
The one and only traitor in our State –
I cannot make myself a traitor too;
So she must die. Well may she pray to Zeus,
The God of Family Love. How, if I tolerate
A traitor at home, shall I rule those abroad?
    He that is a righteous master of his house
Will be a righteous statesman. To trangress
Or twist the law to one's own pleasure, presume
To order where one should obey, is sinful,
And I will have none of it.
He whom the State appoints must be obeyed
To the smallest matter, be it right – or wrong.
And he that rules his household, without a doubt,
Will make the wisest king, or, for that matter,
The staunchest subject. He will be the man
You can depend on in the storm of war,
The faithfullest comrade in the day of battle.
There is no more deadly peril than disobedience;
States are devoured by it, homes laid in ruins,
Armies defeated, victory turned to rout.
While simple obedience saves the lives of hundreds
Of honest folk. Therefore, I hold to the law,
And will never betray it – least of all for a woman.
Better be beaten, if need be, by a man,
Than let a woman get the better of us.

CHORUS: To me, as far as an old man can tell,
It seems your Majesty has spoken well.

HAEMON: Father, man's wisdom is the gift of heaven,
The greatest gift of all. I neither am
Nor wish to be clever enough to prove you wrong,
Though all men might not think the same as you do.
Nevertheless, I have to be your watchdog,

To know what others say and what they do,
And what they find to praise and what to blame.
Your frown is a sufficient silencer
Of any word that is not for your ears.
But *I* hear whispers spoken in the dark;
On every side I hear voices of pity
For this poor girl, doomed to the cruellest death,
And most unjust, that ever woman suffered
For an honourable action – burying a brother
Who was killed in battle, rather than leave him naked
For dogs to maul and carrion birds to peck at.
Has she not rather earned a crown of gold? –
Such is the secret talk about the town.

Father, there is nothing I can prize above
Your happiness and well-being. What greater good
Can any son desire? Can any father
Desire more from his son? Therefore I say,
Let not your first thought be your only thought.
Think if there cannot be some other way.
Surely, to think your own the only wisdom,
And yours the only word, the only will,
Betrays a shallow spirit, an empty heart.
It is no weakness for the wisest man
To learn when he is wrong, know when to yield.
So, on the margin of a flooded river
Trees bending to the torrent live unbroken,
While those that strain against it are snapped off.
A sailor has to tack and slacken sheets
Before the gale, or find himself capsized.

So, father, pause, and put aside your anger.
I think, for what my young opinion's worth,
That, good as it is to have infallible wisdom,
Since this is rarely found, the next best thing
Is to be willing to listen to wise advice.

CHORUS:
There is something to be said, my lord, for his point of view,

And for yours as well; there is much to be said on both sides.

CREON: Indeed! Am I to take lessons at my time of life
From a fellow of his age?

HAEMON: No lesson you need be ashamed of.
It isn't a question of age, but of right and wrong.

CREON:
Would you call it right to admire an act of disobedience?

HAEMON: Not if the act were also dishonourable.

CREON: And was not this woman's action dishonourable?

HAEMON: The people of Thebes think not.

CREON: The people of Thebes!
Since when do I take my orders from the people of Thebes?

HAEMON: Isn't that rather a childish thing to say?

CREON: No. I am king, and responsible only to myself.

HAEMON: A one-man state? What sort of a state is that?

CREON: Why, does not every state belong to its ruler?

HAEMON: You'd be an excellent king – on a desert island.

CREON: Of course, if you're on the woman's side –

HAEMON: No, no –
Unless you're the woman. It's you I'm fighting for.

CREON:
What, villain, when every word you speak is against me?

HAEMON: Only because I know you are wrong, wrong.

CREON: Wrong? To respect my own authority?

HAEMON: What sort of respect tramples on all that is holy?

CREON: Despicable coward! No more will than a woman!

HAEMON: I have nothing to be ashamed of.

CREON: Yet you plead her cause.

HAEMON:
No, *yours*, and mine, and that of the gods of the dead.

CREON: You'll never marry her this side of death.

HAEMON: Then, if she dies, she does not die alone.

CREON: Is that a threat, you impudent –

HAEMON: Is it a threat
To try to argue against wrong-headedness?

CREON: You'll learn what wrong-headedness is, my friend,
     to your cost.

HAEMON:
   O father, I could call you mad, were you not my father.

CREON: Don't toady me, boy; keep that for your lady-love.

HAEMON: You mean to have the last word, then?

CREON: I do.
   And what is more, by all the gods in heaven,
   I'll make you sorry for your impudence.
   (*Calling to those within*)
   Bring out that she-devil, and let her die
   Now, with her bridegroom by to see it done!

HAEMON: That sight I'll never see. Nor from this hour
   Shall you see me again. Let those that will
   Be witness of your wickedness and folly.

Exit.

CHORUS: He is gone, my lord, in very passionate haste.
   And who shall say what a young man's wrath may do?

CREON: Let him go! Let him do! Let him rage as never man
   He shall not save those women from their doom.   [raged,

CHORUS: You mean, then, sire, to put them both to death?

CREON: No, not the one whose hand was innocent.

CHORUS: And to what death do you condemn the other?

CREON: I'll have her taken to a desert place
   Where no man ever walked, and there walled up
   Inside a cave, alive, with food enough
   To acquit ourselves of the blood-guiltiness
   That else would lie upon our commonwealth.
   There she may pray to Death, the god she loves,
   And ask release from death; or learn at last
   What hope there is for those who worship death.

Exit.

CHORUS:
   Where is the equal of Love?
   Where is the battle he cannot win,
   The power he cannot outmatch?

In the farthest corners of earth, in the midst of the sea,
He is there; he is here
In the bloom of a fair face
Lying in wait;
And the grip of his madness
Spares not god or man,

   Marring the righteous man,
Driving his soul into mazes of sin
And strife, dividing a house.
For the light that burns in the eyes of a bride of desire
Is a fire that consumes.
At the side of the great gods
Aphrodite immortal
Works her will upon all.

   The doors are opened and ANTIGONE *enters, guarded.*
But here is a sight beyond all bearing,
At which my eyes cannot but weep;
Antigone forth faring
To her bridal-bower of endless sleep.

ANTIGONE: You see me, countrymen, on my last journey,
   Taking my last leave of the light of day;
   Going to my rest, where death shall take me
   Alive across the silent river.
   No wedding-day; no marriage-music;
   Death will be all my bridal dower.

CHORUS: But glory and praise go with you, lady,
   To your resting-place. You go with your beauty
   Unmarred by the hand of consuming sickness,
   Untouched by the sword, living and free,
   As none other that ever died before you.

ANTIGONE: The daughter of Tantalus, a Phrygian maid,
   Was doomed to a piteous death on the rock
   Of Sipylus, which embraced and imprisoned her,
   Merciless as the ivy; rain and snow
   Beat down upon her, mingled with her tears,

As she wasted and died. Such was her story,
And such is the sleep that I shall go to.

CHORUS: She was a goddess of immortal birth,
And we are mortals; the greater the glory,
To share the fate of a god-born maiden,
A living death, but a name undying.

ANTIGONE: Mockery, mockery! By the gods of our fathers,
Must you make me a laughing-stock while I yet live?
O lordly sons of my city! O Thebes!
Your valleys of rivers, your chariots and horses!
No friend to weep at my banishment
To a rock-hewn chamber of endless durance,
In a strange cold tomb alone to linger
Lost between life and death for ever.

CHORUS: My child, you have gone your way
To the outermost limit of daring
And have stumbled against Law enthroned.
This is the expiation
You must make for the sin of your father.

ANTIGONE: My father – the thought that sears my soul –
The unending burden of the house of Labdacus.
Monstrous marriage of mother and son ...
My father ... my parents ... O hideous shame!
Whom now I follow, unwed, curse-ridden,
Doomed to this death by the ill-starred marriage
That marred my brother's life.

CHORUS: An act of homage is good in itself, my daughter;
But authority cannot afford to connive at disobedience.
You are the victim of your own self-will.

ANTIGONE: And must go the way that lies before me.
No funeral hymn; no marriage-music;
No sun from this day forth, no light,
No friend to weep at my departing.

Enter CREON.

CREON: Weeping and wailing at the door of death!
There'd be no end of it, if it had force

To buy death off. Away with her at once,
And close her up in her rock-vaulted tomb.
Leave her and let her die, if die she must,
Or live within her dungeon. Though on earth
Her life is ended from this day, her blood
Will not be on our hands.

ANTIGONE: So to my grave,
My bridal-bower, my everlasting prison,
I go, to join those many of my kinsmen
Who dwell in the mansions of Persephone,
Last and unhappiest, before my time.
Yet I believe my father will be there
To welcome me, my mother greet me gladly,
And you, my brother, gladly see me come.
Each one of you my hands have laid to rest,
Pouring the due libations on your graves.
It was by this service to your dear body, Polynices,
I earned the punishment which now I suffer,
Though all good people know it was for your honour.
    O but I would not have done the forbidden thing
For any husband or for any son.
For why? I could have had another husband
And by him other sons, if one were lost;
But, father and mother lost, where would I get
Another brother? For thus preferring you,
My brother, Creon condemns me and hales me away,
Never a bride, never a mother, unfriended,
Condemned alive to solitary death.
What law of heaven have I transgressed? What god
Can save me now? What help or hope have I,
In whom devotion is deemed sacrilege?
If this is God's will, I shall learn my lesson
In death; but if my enemies are wrong,
I wish them no worse punishment than mine.

CHORUS: Still the same tempest in the heart
Torments her soul with angry gusts.

CREON: The more cause then have they that guard her
   To hasten their work; or they too suffer.
CHORUS; Alas, that word had the sound of death.
CREON: Indeed there is no more to hope for.
ANTIGONE: Gods of our fathers, my city, my home,
   Rulers of Thebes! Time stays no longer.
   Last daughter of your royal house
   Go I, *his* prisoner, because I honoured
   Those things to which honour truly belongs.

            ANTIGONE *is led away.*

CHORUS*:
   Such was the fate, my child, of Danae
   Locked in a brazen bower,
   A prison secret as a tomb,
   Where was no day.
   Daughter of kings, her royal womb
   Garnered the golden shower
   Of life from Zeus. So strong is Destiny,
   No wealth, no armoury, no tower,
   No ship that rides the angry sea
   Her mastering hand can stay.

    And Dryas' son, the proud Edonian king,
   Pined in a stony cell
   At Dionysus' bidding pent
   To cool his fire
   Till, all his full-blown passion spent,
   He came to know right well
   What god his ribald tongue was challenging
   When he would break the fiery spell
   Of the wild Maenads' revelling
   And vex the Muses' choir.

    It was upon the side
   Of Bosporus, where the Black Rocks stand
   By Thracian Salmydessus over the twin tide,

           * See also p. 168.

That Thracian Ares laughed to see
How Phineus' angry wife most bloodily
Blinded his two sons' eyes that mutely cried
For vengeance; crazed with jealousy
The woman smote them with the weaving-needle in her
                                          [hand.
    Forlorn they wept away
Their sad step-childhood's misery
Predestined from their mother's ill-starred marriage-day.
She was of old Erechtheid blood,
Cave-dwelling daughter of the North-wind God;
On rocky steeps, as mountain ponies play,
The wild winds nursed her maidenhood.
On her, my child, the grey Fates laid hard hands, as upon
    thee.

Enter TEIRESIAS, *the blind prophet, led by a boy.*

TEIRESIAS:
    Gentlemen of Thebes, we greet you, my companion and I,
    Who share one pair of eyes on our journeys together –
    For the blind man goes where his leader tells him to.
CREON:
    You are welcome, father Teiresias. What's your news?
TEIRESIAS: Ay, news you shall have; and advice, if you can
CREON: [heed it.
    There was never a time when I failed to heed it, father.
TEIRESIAS: And thereby have so far steered a steady course.
CREON: And gladly acknowledge the debt we owe to you.
TEIRESIAS:
    Then mark me now; for you stand on a razor's edge.
CREON: Indeed? Grave words from your lips, good priest.
    Say on.
TEIRESIAS: I will; and show you all that my skill reveals.
    At my seat of divination, where I sit
    These many years to read the signs of heaven,
    An unfamiliar sound came to my ears
    Of birds in vicious combat, savage cries

In strange outlandish language, and the whirr
Of flapping wings; from which I well could picture
The gruesome warfare of their deadly talons.
Full of foreboding then I made the test
Of sacrifice upon the altar fire.
There was no answering flame; only rank juice
Oozed from the flesh and dripped among the ashes,
Smouldering and sputtering; the gall vanished in a puff,
And the fat ran down and left the haunches bare.
Thus (through the eyes of my young acolyte,
Who sees for me, that I may see for others)
I read the signs of failure in my quest.
   And why? The blight upon us is *your* doing.
The blood that stains our altars and our shrines,
The blood that dogs and vultures have licked up,
It is none other than the blood of Oedipus
Spilled from the veins of his ill-fated son.
Our fires, our sacrifices, and our prayers
The gods abominate. How should the birds
Give any other than ill-omened voices,
Gorged with the dregs of blood that man has shed?
Mark this, my son: all men fall into sin.
But sinning, he is not for ever lost
Hapless and helpless, who can make amends
And has not set his face against repentance.
Only a fool is governed by self-will.
   Pay to the dead his due. Wound not the fallen.
It is no glory to kill and kill again.
My words are for your good, as is my will,
And should be acceptable, being for your good.
CREON: You take me for your target, reverend sir,
Like all the rest. I know your art of old,
And how you make me your commodity
To trade and traffic in for your advancement.
Trade as you will; but all the silver of Sardis
And all the gold of India will not buy

A tomb for yonder traitor. No. Let the eagles
Carry his carcase up to the throne of Zeus;
Even that would not be sacrilege enough
To frighten me from my determination
Not to allow this burial. No man's act
Has power enough to pollute the goodness of God.
But great and terrible is the fall, Teiresias,
Of mortal men who seek their own advantage
By uttering evil in the guise of good.

TEIRESIAS: Ah, is there any wisdom in the world?

CREON: Why, what is the meaning of that wide-flung taunt?

TEIRESIAS:
What prize outweighs the priceless worth of prudence?

CREON:
Ay, what indeed? What mischief matches the lack of it?

TEIRESIAS: And there you speak of your own symptom, sir.

CREON: I am loth to pick a quarrel with you, priest.

TEIRESIAS: You do so, calling my divination false.

CREON: I say all prophets seek their own advantage.

TEIRESIAS: All kings, say I, seek gain unrighteously.

CREON: Do you forget to whom you say it?

TEIRESIAS: No.
Our king and benefactor, by my guidance.

CREON: Clever you may be, but not therefore honest.

TEIRESIAS: Must I reveal my yet unspoken mind?

CREON: Reveal all; but expect no gain from it.

TEIRESIAS: Does that still seem to you my motive, then?

CREON: Nor is my will for sale, sir, in your market.

TEIRESIAS: Then hear this. Ere the chariot of the sun
Has rounded once or twice his wheeling way,
You shall have given a son of your own loins
To death, in payment for death – two debts to pay:
One for the life that you have sent to death,
The life you have abominably entombed;
One for the dead still lying above ground
Unburied, unhonoured, unblest by the gods below.

You cannot alter this. The gods themselves
Cannot undo it. It follows of necessity
From what you have done. Even now the avenging Furies,
The hunters of Hell that follow and destroy,
Are lying in wait for you, and will have their prey,
When the evil you have worked for others falls on you.
Do I speak this for my gain? The time shall come,
And soon, when your house will be filled with the lamenta-
Of men and of women; and every neighbouring city [tion
Will be goaded to fury against you, for upon them
Too the pollution falls when the dogs and vultures
Bring the defilement of blood to their hearths and altars.
   I have done. You pricked me, and these shafts of wrath
Will find their mark in your heart. You cannot escape
The sting of their sharpness.
Lead me home, my boy.
Let us leave him to vent his anger on younger ears,
Or school his mind and tongue to a milder mood
Than that which now possesses him.
Lead on.

Exit.

CHORUS:
  He has gone, my lord. He has prophesied terrible things.
  And for my part, I that was young and now am old
  Have never known his prophecies proved false.

CREON: It is true enough; and my heart is torn in two.
  It is hard to give way, and hard to stand and abide
  The coming of the curse. Both ways are hard.

CHORUS: If you would be advised, my good lord Creon –

CREON: What must I do? Tell me, and I will do it.

CHORUS: Release the woman from her rocky prison.
  Set up a tomb for him that lies unburied.

CREON: Is it your wish that I consent to this?

CHORUS: It is, and quickly. The gods do not delay
  The stroke of their swift vengeance on the sinner.

CREON: It is hard, but I must do it. Well I know

There is no armour against necessity.

CHORUS: Go. Let your own hand do it, and no other.

CREON: I will go this instant.
Slaves there! One and all.
Bring spades and mattocks out on the hill!
My mind is made; 'twas I imprisoned her,
And I will set her free. Now I believe
It is by the laws of heaven that man must live.

Exit.

CHORUS:
O Thou whose name is many,
Son of the Thunderer, dear child of his Cadmean bride,
Whose hand is mighty
In Italia,
In the hospitable valley
Of Eleusis,
And in Thebes,
The mother-city of thy worshippers,
Where sweet Ismenus gently watereth
The soil whence sprang the harvest of the dragon's teeth;

Where torches on the crested mountains gleam,
And by Castalia's stream
The nymph-train in thy dance rejoices,
When from the ivy-tangled glens
Of Nysa and from vine-clad plains
Thou comest to Thebes where the immortal voices
Sing thy glad strains.

Thebes, where thou lovest most to be,
With her, thy mother, the fire-stricken one,
Sickens for need of thee.
Healer of all her ills;
Come swiftly o'er the high Parnassian hills,
Come o'er the sighing sea.

The stars, whose breath is fire, delight
To dance for thee; the echoing night

Shall with thy praises ring.
Zeus-born, appear! With Thyiads revelling
Come, bountiful
Iacchus, King!

Enter a MESSENGER, *from the side of the stage.*

MESSENGER: Hear, men of Cadmus' city, hear and attend,
   Men of the house of Amphion, people of Thebes!
   What is the life of man? A thing not fixed
   For good or evil, fashioned for praise or blame.
   Chance raises a man to the heights, chance casts him down,
   And none can foretell what will be from what is.
   Creon was once an enviable man;
   He saved his country from her enemies,
   Assumed the sovereign power, and bore it well,
   The honoured father of a royal house.
   Now all is lost; for life without life's joys
   Is living death; and such a life is his.
   Riches and rank and show of majesty
   And state, where no joy is, are empty, vain
   And unsubstantial shadows, of no weight
   To be compared with happiness of heart.
CHORUS: What is your news? Disaster in the royal house?
MESSENGER: Death; and the guilt of it on living heads.
CHORUS: Who dead? And by what hand?
MESSENGER: Haemon is dead,
   Slain by his own –
CHORUS: His father?
MESSENGER: His own hand.
   His father's act it was that drove him to it.
CHORUS: Then all has happened as the prophet said.
MESSENGER: What's next to do, your worships will decide.
           The Palace door opens.
CHORUS: Here comes the Queen, Eurydice. Poor soul,
   It may be she has heard about her son.
        Enter EURYDICE, *attended by women.*

EURYDICE:

My friends, I heard something of what you were saying
As I came to the door. I was on my way to prayer
At the temple of Pallas, and had barely turned the latch
When I caught your talk of some near calamity.
I was sick with fear and reeled in the arms of my women.
But tell me what is the matter; what have you heard?
I am not unacquainted with grief, and I can bear it.

MESSENGER:

Madam, it was I that saw it, and will tell you all.
To try to make it any lighter now
Would be to prove myself a liar. Truth
Is always best.
It was thus. I attended your husband,
The King, to the edge of the field where lay the body
Of Polynices, in pitiable state, mauled by the dogs.
We prayed for him to the Goddess of the Roads, and to Pluto,
That they might have mercy upon him. We washed the [remains
In holy water, and on a fire of fresh-cut branches
We burned all that was left of him, and raised
Over his ashes a mound of his native earth.
That done, we turned towards the deep rock-chamber
Of the maid that was married with death.
Before we reached it,
One that stood near the accursed place had heard
Loud cries of anguish, and came to tell King Creon.
As he approached, came strange uncertain sounds
Of lamentation, and he cried aloud:
'Unhappy wretch! Is my foreboding true?
Is this the most sorrowful journey that ever I went?
My son's voice greets me. Go, some of you, quickly
Through the passage where the stones are thrown apart,
Into the mouth of the cave, and see if it be
My son, my own son Haemon that I hear.
If not, I am the sport of gods.'
We went

And looked, as bidden by our anxious master.
There in the furthest corner of the cave
We saw her hanging by the neck. The rope
Was of the woven linen of her dress.
And, with his arms about her, there stood he
Lamenting his lost bride, his luckless love,
His father's cruelty.
When Creon saw them,
Into the cave he went, moaning piteously.
'O my unhappy boy,' he cried again,
'What have you done? What madness brings you here
To your destruction? Come away, my son,
My son, I do beseech you, come away!'
His son looked at him with one angry stare,
Spat in his face, and then without a word
Drew sword and struck out. But his father fled
Unscathed. Whereon the poor demented boy
Leaned on his sword and thrust it deeply home
In his own side, and while his life ebbed out
Embraced the maid in loose-enfolding arms,
His spurting blood staining her pale cheeks red.

      EURYDICE *goes quickly back into the Palace.*

Two bodies lie together, wedded in death,
Their bridal sleep a witness to the world
How great calamity can come to man
Through man's perversity.
CHORUS: But what is this?
The Queen has turned and gone without a word.
MESSENGER: Yes. It is strange. The best that I can hope
Is that she would not sorrow for her son
Before us all, but vents her grief in private
Among her women. She is too wise, I think,
To take a false step rashly.
CHORUS: It may be.
Yet there is danger in unnatural silence
No less than in excess of lamentation.

MESSENGER: I will go in and see, whether in truth
 There is some fatal purpose in her grief.
 Such silence, as you say, may well be dangerous.
     He goes in.
  Enter Attendants preceding the King.
CHORUS: The King comes here.
 What the tongue scarce dares to tell
 Must now be known
 By the burden that proves too well
 The guilt, no other man's
 But his alone.
   Enter CREON *with the body of* HAEMON.
CREON: The sin, the sin of the erring soul
 Drives hard unto death.
 Behold the slayer, the slain,
 The father, the son.
 O the curse of my stubborn will!
 Son, newly cut off in the newness of youth,
 Dead for my fault, not yours.
CHORUS: Alas, too late you have seen the truth.
CREON: I learn in sorrow. Upon my head
 God has delivered this heavy punishment,
 Has struck me down in the ways of wickedness,
 And trod my gladness under foot.
 Such is the bitter affliction of mortal man.
   Enter the MESSENGER *from the Palace.*
MESSENGER: Sir, you have this and more than this to bear.
 Within there's more to know, more to your pain.
CREON: What more? What pain can overtop this pain?
MESSENGER:
 She is dead – your wife, the mother of him that is dead –
 The death-wound fresh in her heart. Alas, poor lady!
CREON: Insatiable Death, wilt thou destroy me yet?
 What say you, teller of evil?
 I am already dead,
 And is there more?

Blood upon blood?
More death? My wife?
 The central doors open, revealing the body of EURYDICE.
CHORUS: Look then, and see; nothing is hidden now.
CREON: O second horror!
 What fate awaits me now?
 My child here in my arms ... and there, the other ...
 The son ... the mother ...
MESSENGER: There at the altar with the whetted knife
 She stood, and as the darkness dimmed her eyes
 Called on the dead, her elder son and this,
 And with her dying breath cursed you, their slayer.
CREON: O horrible ...
 Is there no sword for me,
 To end this misery?
MESSENGER: Indeed you bear the burden of two deaths.
 It was her dying word.
CREON: And her last act?
MESSENGER: Hearing her son was dead, with her own hand
 She drove the sharp sword home into her heart.
CREON: There is no man can bear this guilt but I.
 It is true, I killed him.
 Lead me away, away. I live no longer.
CHORUS: 'Twere best, if anything is best in evil times.
 What's soonest done, is best, when all is ill.
CREON: Come, my last hour and fairest,
 My only happiness ... come soon.
 Let me not see another day.
 Away ... away ...
CHORUS: The future is not to be known; our present care
 Is with the present; the rest is in other hands.
CREON: I ask no more than I have asked.
CHORUS: Ask nothing.
 What is to be, no mortal can escape.
CREON: I am nothing. I have no life.
 Lead me away ...

That have killed unwittingly
My son, my wife.
I know not where I should turn,
Where look for help.
My hands have done amiss, my head is bowed
With fate too heavy for me.

Exit.

CHORUS: Of happiness the crown
And chiefest part
Is wisdom, and to hold
The gods in awe.
This is the law
That, seeing the stricken heart
Of pride brought down,
We learn when we are old.

EXEUNT

NOTES TO 'KING OEDIPUS'

P. 25   *Branches and garlands:* branches of olive or laurel, festooned with wool, are carried by the suppliants or laid on the altars.

P. 27   *The Pythian House of Apollo:* the temple at Delphi, where the oracles of Apollo were given by the 'Pythian' priestess.

P. 28   *Phoebus:* Apollo. Other names for the god are: Loxias, the Lycean god, the Healer. He is both the author of the divine messages (which at the same time are the messages of Zeus, the God of gods) and the source of help and relief, the slayer of evil things.

P. 31   *Bacchus:* also called Dionysus, and other names; not only the god in whose honour the Athenian festival of tragedy is held, but also especially related, in legend and cult, to Thebes.

P. 33   *Chorus:* lines so allotted in the dialogue are, of course, spoken only by one member, usually the leader.

P. 38   *Let him take you home:* some think that Oedipus should leave the stage, unknown to Teiresias, before the latter's last speech – on the ground that the purport of this speech must otherwise be unmistakeable to Oedipus. But does Teiresias reveal much more than he has already said? The producer will decide; but should guard against a possible comic effect in Teiresias' speaking to the air.

P. 39   *Heart of Earth:* the Delphic temple, spoken of as the centre, or navel, of earth.

P. 43   *Consent, O King, consent:* these twenty-one lines of lyrical dialogue, answered by twenty-one corresponding lines at 'Persuade, Madam, persuade', represent fairly closely the 'kommos' of the original – a form used in passages of heightened emotion, anger, or grief, at least once in every play. The producer should contrive some stylistic method of marking the change of *tempo*.

P. 50   *Tokens of supplication:* garlanded branches like those carried by the suppliants. Jocasta's reappearance on this pious errand is in marked contrast to her recent words, and strikes sharply against the Chorus's forebodings about the decline of reverence.

     Messenger: an elderly man; and not a mere message-carrier, but something of an ambassador. Risen from humble station to a position of trust, and now charged with an important mission, he is complacent and not a little patronizing. Beneath the light surface of his scene a discovery of shattering significance is about to be made. Note the subtle tragi-comic cross-currents in his confidence that his news is good because (*a*) Oedipus's 'father' is dead, and (*b*) Meropé is not his mother. The dreadful contradiction is not his concern.

P. 54   *Was I found, or bought?* The correct reading may be 'Was I your son, or bought?' This has the advantage of increasing the surprise of the Messenger's answer 'Found'; but could Oedipus have ignored, or disbelieved, the explicit statement of a few lines above?

P. 55   *What does it matter?* At what point in the scene does Jocasta guess the whole truth? 'Cithaeron', 'ankles', 'shepherd', have driven daggers into her heart, and she is now at the extremity of her endurance.

P. 56   *Chorus:* suspecting nothing but good in the discovery, or seeking to put the most hopeful construction on it, they anticipate a romantic and supernatural explanation. Oedipus and the Corinthian presumably remain on the stage during these lines.
         Cyllene's lord: Hermes.

P. 61   *Eyes that should see no longer:* these 'wild and whirling words' are intentionally obscure in the original. In cold blood they mean that his eyes 'should no longer see those he should never have seen (his children), nor go on failing to recognize (as they had hitherto done) those he would have liked to see (his parents), but for both offences be blinded for ever'.

P. 63   *Twice tormented …:* the Greek means either 'Unhappy man, both in your physical and mental suffering, I wish I had never known you' or '… I wish you had never known', *i.e.* found out the terrible truth. I prefer the latter sense, for, though the other is a possible sentiment in the mouth of the Chorus (and has, in fact, been used once already: *p.* 59), its repetition here seems both weak and harsh; while the alternative rendering contains a key to the theme of the play: the physical agony of Oedipus is but the counterpart to the spiritual torture of self-knowledge.

P. 72   *Dread goddesses:* these beings, whose influence looms large throughout this play, are variously described. Their most common title of *Eumenides* ('Kindly Ones') is perhaps partly a euphemism, adopted in fearful veneration, but also signifies their power of protection for the innocent (or penitent), the converse of their vengeance on the guilty. Even their vengeance is of the nature of a purification of the guilty conscience, through suffering and self-knowledge, leading to a merciful resolution of conflict. Sophocles adopts a traditional association of these divinities with Colonus, using it to reinforce another central theme of the play – the Athenian tradition of justice tempered with mercy.

P. 75   *Chorus:* the chorus of this play take an unusually prominent part in the action and dialogue. Much of the latter must clearly be assigned to the leader, though occasional lines may conveniently be given to other individual members.

P. 81   *Ismene:* it seems likely that she is the elder of the two sisters, though I don't know that this is anywhere specified. Both here and in *Antigone* she is the 'Martha' of the pair – the more practical but less sensitive.

P. 92   *The olive:* in historical times the most valuable commercial asset of Attica, it is here credited with fabulous origin and divine protection. As to its invulnerability, legend received the support of history, when the Spartan invaders of Attica during the years 431–421 B.C. spared the sacred olive-groves out of a common regard for the majesty of Athena.

P. 93   *Poseidon,* whose special patronage of Colonus and Athens is noticed at various points in this play, combines, rather curiously, the tutelage both of the sea and of horses, and to his guidance is attributed the Athenian skill with ship and horse. In point of fact, most thriving Greek communities seem to have liked to describe their lands as 'rich in horses', and those which also had access to the sea naturally looked on seamanship and horsemanship as twin and complementary factors in human achievement; hence, perhaps, their ascription to the same god.

P. 96   *Or you and I must fight:* if the Chorus seem unaccountably helpless in spite of their loud protests, we must remember (1) that Creon is heavily guarded, at least until Antigone is taken off, (2) even when alone, the sanctity of his kingship perhaps protects him from physical assault, (3) the convention and construction of the stage may have prohibited actual contact between chorus and actors. The scene is thus at a deadlock, Creon threatening but not actually invading the sanctuary which protects Oedipus, and the Chorus threatening attack on Creon – when Theseus enters to command the attention of all. Such conflicts were usually expressed in verbal duel, sharpened by symmetry of metre and phrase.

P. 100   *Hill of Ares:* the Areiopagus, from immemorial time the seat of the ancient council of Athens.

P. 103   *Pythian shrine:* a temple of Apollo on the road leading to the sea-coast.

　　　　　hallowed sand: the same coast, in the neighbourhood of Eleusis, where the rites of Demeter were celebrated.

P. 104   *White Oea:* on the alternative hill-route which the fugitives may have taken.

P. 113   *Father of Darkness:* the Greek is 'paternal darkness of Hades'; variously interpreted also as 'the darkness in which Laius lies', or 'a darkness like that of your father's eyes'.

P. 117   *And no one else must know it:* strictly speaking, it is the *grave* of Oedipus, not the *place of his death,* that is to be known to Theseus alone; the latter is indeed described almost precisely by the Messenger. Either the author is guilty of a slight inconsistency here, or we are to allow that Oedipus is not supposed to have a complete prevision of his final moments and the ultimate disposal of his remains.

P. 123   *And where shall I be safe?* From here to the entrance of Theseus, the principal MS authority leaves us in doubt as to the names of the speakers, and we are free to choose whether it is Antigone or Ismene who holds this dialogue with the Chorus. Dramatic fitness seems to require that Antigone should be left silently intent upon the thought of revisiting her father's grave (the subject she immediately reintroduces on the arrival of Theseus), while Ismene, characteristically, is concerned about her own and her sister's future. Most editors, however, have given the lines to Antigone, though Jebb admits the fitness of assigning them to Ismene.

NOTES TO 'ANTIGONE'

P. 128   *How our father perished:* there is no reference here to the events of *Oedipus at Colonus*, and a later speech of Antigone (*p.* 150) even more explicitly contradicts them. There were, in fact, varying versions of the legend, and in the present play Sophocles is using the oldest tradition, by which Oedipus died at Thebes, perhaps shortly after his wife's suicide.

P. 149   *Ill-starred marriage:* the marriage of Polynices to the Argive princess, the token of the alliance that made possible his fatal attack on Thebes.

P. 150   *O but I would not have done the forbidden thing:* the following nine lines, possibly a spurious interpolation, are rejected by some editors as being both logically and psychologically inappropriate. On the supposition that Antigone, in her last despair, gives utterance to an inconsistent and even unworthy thought, the passage seems to me to be dramatically right.

P. 156   *O Thou whose name is many:* believing the solution of their troubles to be now in sight, the Chorus invoke Iacchus (*alias* Bacchus, Dionysus, and other 'many names') as being (1) particularly connected with Thebes, (2) giver of healing and release.

P. 158   *I attended your husband:* it is not by an oversight that the Messenger's narrative places first the attention given by Creon to the body of Polynices, and second his attempt to release Antigone. Though the king left the stage declaring his intention to save the woman's life, it is the wrong done to the dead that lies heaviest on his conscience. We misread the intention of the tragedy if we place at its centre the 'martyrdom' of Antigone; for the Athenian audience its first theme is the retribution brought upon Creon for his defiance of sacred obligations, a retribution in which Antigone and Haemon incidentally share.

*

The following alternative rendering of the 'Danae' Chorus (p. 151) may be found more acceptable for dramatic performance. The mythological complexities of the original have here been considerably simplified in order to bring out the essential theme of the ode – precedents for the fate of Antigone.

So, long ago, lay Danae
   Entombed within her brazen bower;
Noble and beautiful was she,
   On whom there fell the golden shower
   Of life from Zeus. There is no tower
So high, no armoury so great,
   No ship so swift, as is the power
Of man's inexorable fate.

There was the proud Edonian king,
   Lycurgus, in rock-prison pent
For arrogantly challenging
   God's laws: it was his punishment
   Of that swift passion to repent
In slow perception, for that he
   Had braved the rule omnipotent
Of Dionysus' sovereignty.

On Phineus' wife the hand of fate
   Was heavy, when her children fell
Victims to a stepmother's hate,
   And she endured a prison-cell
   Where the North Wind stood sentinel
In caverns amid mountains wild.
   Thus the grey spinners wove their spell
On her, as upon thee, my child.